# *Risky Shot*

## Book 2 in the Bluegrass Series

Kathleen Brooks

# Books by Kathleen Brooks

## Bluegrass Series

Bluegrass State of Mind

Risky Shot

Dead Heat

## Bluegrass Brothers Series

Bluegrass Undercover

Rising Storm

Secret Santa, A Bluegrass Series Novella

Acquiring Trouble

Relentless Pursuit

Secrets Collide

# Prologue

---

Danielle De Luca pulled her rusting-out, muffler-dragging, piece-of-shit Chevy Lumina off to the side of the road and rested her head against the wheel. Well, more like banged her head against the wheel — repeatedly.

Dani took in a deep breath and felt a river of sweat run down her back as she peeled her shirt from the seat. She reached across the stick shift and grabbed the gallon jug of water for her radiator. She popped her hood and watched the hot steam erupt. It wouldn't surprise her if steam were coming out of her ears, too. This trip had been a nightmare. Between looking over her shoulder for the men in black suits or her car deciding to do its imitation of a geyser, a twelve-hour trip turned into a sixteen-hour one.

Waiting for the steam to stop, she placed her hands on her trim hips and looked around. She was on a narrow country road outside of Lexington, Kentucky, heading toward her friend living in Keeneston. She wiped her wet palm on her khaki shorts and pulled up her white ribbed tank top to wipe the beads of sweat from her forehead. The only thing she saw around her was a couple cows munching grass and staring at her.

The heat was oppressive. She couldn't believe that air could feel heavy this early in the morning. She had grown up in the cool mountains of Northern Italy and then spent her teenage years in

Milo, Maine. Neither place had prepared her for the humidity of Kentucky near the end of June.

Even though Kentucky was hot, she did have to admit it was pretty. The field the cows were in had gently rolling hills outlined by black four-board fences and sprinkled with a wide range of big leafy trees, not the fir trees she was used to in Maine. The grass gave the impression that it was an ocean of blue-green color dancing in the wind while the cows lazily enjoyed it.

Looking back at her car, she grabbed the water jug and cautiously approached her radiator. She quickly tapped the top of it with her middle finger, pulling it back quickly when it burned her finger. She pried open her back door and rummaged around until she came up with an old bandanna to use to wrench open the radiator cap. She poured in the last of the water and hoped it was enough to get her to Keeneston.

Dani tightened the cap and was about to close the hood when she heard a car pull over in the grass behind her. She placed her hand in her pocket and felt the cool steel of her knife. Slowly she peeked around the hood and relaxed when she saw the brown sheriff's car parked there. The door opened and a heavy-set man in his sixties got out. He would've had shocking red hair when he was younger, but now it had been dimmed by some gray hair woven throughout.

"Having some trouble there, hon?" He gestured to the open hood.

"No, sir. Well, not any more than normal, that is. I got her all filled up and she should be cool enough in a minute." Dani raised her arms and slammed the hood closed.

"Where ya heading, ma'am? I'll follow you for a bit to make sure you don't get stranded again."

Dani relaxed more and smiled. "I'm actually trying to get to Keeneston. Am I going the right way?"

"You sure are. I'm the sheriff of Keene County."

"Danielle De Luca, it's nice to meet you, Sheriff." She wiped her hand again on her shorts before shaking his hand.

"You can call me Red. Just follow me and I'll lead you right into town." He turned and started back to his car.

She stopped him before he got to his car. "Actually, maybe you could help me. I'm looking for a friend of mine, McKenna Mason. Would you happen to know where to find her?"

She saw Red pause and then raise his hand to stroke his chin. "I don't know if I can recall that name. Do you know where she lives?"

"She gave me two places to look. A bed and breakfast and her boyfriend's house, a Will Ashton, but didn't give me an address for either."

"You say she's your sister?"

"No, I'm her friend, we worked together in New York. She sent me an email telling me to come here. There's something we need to do together…" She stopped explaining herself and decided this country cop wouldn't know where to find his gun if it wasn't strapped onto his waist.

"I know who you are, Miss De Luca, I just needed to make sure it was really you. As you know, it's not the safest for her right now and we look after our own. Kenna's been waiting almost six weeks for you to get here. She's out at Will's. I'll show you the way." Red turned and left her standing open-mouthed by her car as he hoisted himself into his.

She couldn't believe it. She had just gotten played by a country cop. She felt embarrassed about her assumptions but relieved to not have to find her way into town herself.

Red flashed his lights and waved out the window to a driveway on her left. She flashed her lights and waved back before turning into the driveway. An ornate metal gate supported by beautiful gray stone walls stood closed before her. Fields of green spread as far as she could see. Some cows dotted the landscape and a horse that looked to be one hundred years old slowly plodded his way to the fence to stare at her. Keeping an eye on the horse, she stopped at the call box and pushed the button.

The box crackled and then, "Hello?" a woman's nice-sounding Southern voice said.

"Um, hello. I'm here to see Kenna."

"And who should I say is calling?" The voice was still nice, but Dani could hear it take on an edge of suspicion.

"Danielle De Luca."

"Oh! Oh! Dani! Oh, William! Open the gate, Kenna's friend has finally arrived."

Dani chuckled. She couldn't help but like a woman who sounded so kind. The gate opened and Dani drove through. She passed the cows and waved goodbye to the old horse as she drove down the long driveway. She pulled up in front of a huge white mansion and gawked. Maybe raising cows and old horses was very lucrative?

Before she could even turn the engine off, the front door was flung open and an elegant older lady came running out. She had light-blonde hair put up in a perfect ponytail that was held in place by a peach ribbon that matched her sundress. A very tall, handsome man with brown hair followed fondly behind. His hair had just a touch of gray at the temples to show his age.

Dani got out of the car and was encased in the tightest hug she had ever felt. "Oh, you poor, sweet dear. Oh, bless your heart! We're so happy you're finally here."

"Thank you," she managed to gasp out.

"Bets, you're scaring her, or cutting off her air at any rate." The woman released her but kept her hand on her arm. "I'm William Ashton and this is my wife, Betsy."

"Nice to meet you both." Dani smiled at the obvious affection between the Ashtons.

"I bet you can't wait to see Kenna." William put an arm around her shoulder and turned her to face the house. "See that side road there? You'll want to go down that road until it ends. It'll take you a few minutes, so don't worry that you've gone wandering off the wrong way. Go ahead and go right on down. I'm sure you'll catch her before she leaves for work."

"Thank you." She tried to turn and get back into the car but was once more enveloped into another tight hug by Betsy.

"Okay, I'll let you go. You just must promise me you'll stop by again soon. We'll have dinner after you get settled in." Betsy patted her hand one last time and finally let go. Dani waved goodbye and got back into the car.

She drove through the farm, seeing horses, cows, some corn, and lots and lots of land. The Ashtons had been great, but she was still not used to being around people, especially people who touched her.

The past four months had been similar to the show "Man Versus Wild." However, in her version, she wasn't trapped in some nice jungle. She was in New York City, where she often lived out of her car and nearly froze each night. She prayed she wouldn't be carjacked, mugged, or worse. The other nights were spent fighting for room in a shelter where she didn't get any sleep due to crying babies or strange men trying to sneak into her cot. She wished she were in the jungle with Bear Grylls leading her toward civilization. In New York, she didn't have raging currents or dangerous snakes, but she did face danger in the form of men in bad suits carrying guns.

As she drove by more beautiful pastures framed with freshly painted black fences, she grew more and more bitter. "Come on, girl, don't do this." She shook her head and tried to push down the feeling of anger working its way up to the surface. She had been sleeping in her car and Kenna had been living in the lap of luxury. She had been gathering information out of garbage cans while Kenna was getting home-cooked meals and hugs from Betsy.

Dani made herself take a deep breath and let it out slowly. She rounded a corner and went over a hill and her jaw clenched in anger when she saw the most amazing white house sitting in a perfectly landscaped yard flying a blue and white UK flag. All the bitter thoughts came rushing back in. The freezing nights she had slept in her car, the constant worry she'd be caught at any second, ugh! She shook her head to clear her thoughts.

"Relax. Down, green monster, down!" she said to herself as she took nice, long deep breaths. She put the car in gear and made her way to the front door. Ringing the bell, her heart kept pounding louder and louder as she waited for the door to open.

She heard some pounding and finally heels clicked on hardwood seconds before the front door was thrown open. Kenna stood in the doorway, her mouth frozen in the middle of the *H* for hello. Her hair was put up, but her shirt was untucked and her skirt wasn't quite straight.

"Hey, girl. Ready for work?" She grinned, some of the anger burning off. She looked down and saw the purple Pradas she and Kenna had joked about in one of their emails. "Hey! Didn't you promise me those shoes?"

She saw the tears start in Kenna's eyes and was pulled into a fierce hug. She had guessed right, Kenna had been spending a lot of time with Betsy. She hugged her back and guilt washed over her for being so bitter and jealous of Kenna when it was obvious Kenna had been worried about her. However, she was having a hard time banishing all ill thoughts.

Dani pulled back. "So, where can a girl find a place to stay around here?"

Kenna burst out laughing and put an arm over her shoulder. "I know the perfect place."

# Chapter One

Kenna pulled Danielle inside and led her to the kitchen. "Looks like things are going well for you." Dani noticed the granite countertops and brand new, shiny stainless steel appliances as Kenna poured two cups of coffee into new stoneware mugs.

"When one door closes, another one opens. I was just lucky enough to walk through it." Dani watched Kenna talking with her hands and saw the sparkle on her ring finger.

"Whoa, girl! What is that on your finger?" She grabbed Kenna's left hand and stared at the massive emerald-cut engagement ring.

"I'm engaged!" Kenna squealed. "Will asked me just a couple of weeks ago. Now you can be my maid of honor! Please say you will."

Dani smiled and nodded her agreement. They had talked about getting married quite a bit on their lunch breaks or when they were working late. Dani knew even though Kenna was smiling and happy, a piece of her was hurting. One night, she had told Dani that with the happiness of an engagement, the sadness of missing her family would surely come. Jealousy and anger arose within her as she looked around at the cute, cheerful yellow curtains hanging over the windows and the crystal vase filled with roses sitting on the kitchen table. All this time, all this work… and Kenna has been doing nothing. Nothing but hooking some rich man into marriage. No, that's not right. Kenna would never do that. Man, she really needed to get a grip on herself.

"Thank you!" Kenna jumped up and down and gave her another big hug. "I can't wait for you to meet him. He'll be down in a second. But what is more important at this moment is where have you been? I was worried sick about you after I didn't hear from you for six weeks! Are you okay?"

"Yeah, I'm okay. I've been living out of my car more and more and the last couple of months have been pretty busy up there. I didn't want to risk leaving a stakeout place to find a library." Dani took a sip of the coffee and melted. It was the first real cup of coffee she'd had in months. She had pretty much been living off water for weeks now since it was the only thing she could afford.

"Stakeouts? Dani, why did you go through all of that? Living out of your car, tailing men, why?" She watched Kenna's eyes widen at the thought of it.

"Because if no one else did we'd be hiding for the rest of our lives. The police and the FBI are in on this. We'd never be able to hide forever. Since you fled New York, I decided to stay and do it. I wanted to know what I was up against at the very least." Dani pulled out a bar stool and sat. She realized that she sounded pissed, but she was. If she was totally honest, she'd acknowledge that Kenna hadn't asked her to stay in New York. In fact, she had told her to leave. But what she did gave them valuable information and she was ready for this to be over.

"FBI? Do you know who? I've been working with an Agent Cole Parker; did that name come up?" Kenna pulled out the seat and Dani watched as the color drained from her cheeks. Apparently Kenna wasn't as unaffected as she had thought. Guilt's hand started to reach for her and she quickly swatted it away.

"No, I never heard the name Cole Parker before." She took another sip of her coffee and tried not to swallow the whole thing like a shot.

"Good. Like I said, we've been working with him and even though he's a bit of a tight-ass, he seems like a good guy. So tell me what you found out then?" Kenna leaned forward in her seat and Dani couldn't help but notice the way her eyes had narrowed, just like when she was cross-examining someone on the stand.

"I'd rather just go through it once. I assume Agent Parker will want to hear about it, so why don't you set up a meeting with all these people you say are working on this and I'll run through it." The thought of going over and over it again and again brought on a headache. She was tired and had always hated telling the same story over and over to different people. Hopefully, she could get away with one big interrogation and be done with it.

"Of course. That's a great idea. I'll call him now to set it up." She watched Kenna slide off the stool and head over to the phone.

"Kenna! Stop at the barn and have a talk with your Boots! He's refusing to leave the barn again. It's all because of you and your kisses. He has to have one every morning now." Dani stopped drinking her coffee at the sight of the heavily muscled, tall, half-naked man who strode into the kitchen.

"Oh, Will!" Kenna launched herself at the man wearing only a pair of jeans that rode nice and low on his hips. "Dani finally made it!"

She saw him blush when he realized they weren't alone. Slipping on a white t-shirt, he headed over to give her a hug. "I'm so glad you finally made it. We were getting worried about you. Will Ashton, by the way." He held out his hand after he let go of her and she shook it.

She was surprised someone as obviously attractive as Will wasn't strutting around to get her to ogle him. She knew that sounded conceited, but men had a tendency to notice her and act like morons, never caring about anything but her looks. But Will only seemed concerned about what she thought and how comfortable she was. No wonder Kenna said yes so fast. She was happy for her friend. Or at least she would be when she resolved her feelings toward Kenna.

Will was already better than all of her other boyfriends who would hit on Dani when Kenna wasn't around.

"Will, are you free tonight around six?" Kenna asked him.

"Should be done by then, why?" Will stuffed a muffin in his mouth and then offered the box to Dani.

"We're holding a security briefing, so to say. Dani is going to fill us all in on what has been going on in New York. I was just getting ready to call Cole. Do you think you can call him, Ahmed, and Mo on your way to the barn? I want to show Dani the town and take her to Miss Lily's before I have to be in court."

Dani couldn't help but snort. "Miss Lily's? Are you taking me to an old town brothel?"

Will laughed out loud and Kenna tried not to, but failed. "Don't let her hear you say that. Miss Lily Rae Rose and her sisters, Miss Daisy Mae Rose and Miss Violet Fae Rose, have the bed and breakfast and the Blossom Cafe. They'll all in their late sixties, I'd guess, and swear to be good Baptists as they serve the stiffest drink in town! I think of them as the fairy godmothers from *Sleeping Beauty*."

"So I'm staying with one of them?" Dani asked as she grabbed one of the muffins Will had placed in front of her.

"I stayed at the bed and breakfast with Miss Lily up until a couple of weeks ago. It's really nice and the food is excellent." That got Dani's attention. She had already finished the muffin and was reaching for another.

"Come on, grab the muffin and I'll let you drive me to work. I'll show you around town as we go. But first we have to stop by the barn so I can kiss a horse." Kenna reached over the counter and snagged a muffin and headed for the door. Dani was confused about the horse kissing, but the desire for food overrode her curiosity. She thought about going for the last banana nut but decided on the chocolate chip instead. Nothing could beat chocolate disguised as breakfast.

"You two ladies have fun. I'll see you tonight at six." He kissed Kenna as she reached for her purse. "I'm so happy you're here, Dani. I'll see you tonight, too." He leaned over and gave her a brotherly type peck on the head. The action was enough to almost get her to cry. Four months of depending on no one and suddenly she felt like she had a sister and now a brother looking out for her.

"I can't believe this car survived hitting Chad and is still going? How did I not hear the muffler when you pulled up?" Kenna laughed as Dani drove them into town. Dani drove past more cows, more black fences, and more corn until she could see the tops of building. "Okay, you're going to turn here and *voila*, you're on Main Street."

"This is Main Street? Where's the traffic?" She peered out her dirty windshield and only saw a street with American flags on every light pole, overflowing flower baskets right under them, and benches on the sidewalk. "Where are the traffic lights? Where's the rest of the town?" She started down the street toward the courthouse and church peeking out.

"Well, there's one and there's the other," Kenna laughed as she pointed to the two stoplights. Kenna then gestured to her right. "And this is the town! That's my friend Paige's store." She pointed to the left. "And that is where my law firm is."

After just a couple of blocks, an old courthouse came into view. It was a four-storied, square limestone structure that looked really old. In the front of the courthouse, a large statue of Lady Justice sat astride a horse. Flowerpots were planted and lined the sidewalk leading toward the large double door in the front. "You can let me off here. This is obviously the courthouse. On the other side of the street is the Blossom Cafe. Let's meet there for lunch today. How about twelve-thirty?" Dani nodded her agreement but Kenna was already talking again. "Then at the second stoplight, turn right and go up the hill. Miss Lily's is the Victorian on your right with the great porch." Kenna stopped with her hand on the door. "Dani, it's really great you're here. I know together we can get through this thing."

Kenna surprised her by launching herself over the stick shift and squeezing tight. Betsy was really rubbing off on her. "Thanks, Kenna. It's going to be hard. But you're right, we need to do it. Have fun in court. I'll see you later."

She watched Kenna get out of the car, waving and talking to all the people walking into the courthouse through a glass door on the side. Kenna had found a new home. She wondered if she could, too.

She stopped her car in front of the big white Victorian and stared. Kenna was right, it had a great porch. There were white wicker chairs with pale green cushions that looked thick enough to sink into and never come out, but it was the big porch swing that caught her eye. It could hold three people and was anchored in such a way that you could see down to a great little flower garden.

As she walked up the front stairs to the freshly painted green door, she had to fight the urge to curl up and take a nap in the swing. Before she could ring the bell, the door opened and a little woman with beauty-parlor-permed white hair stood before her.

"Yes? Can I help you, dear?" The woman's Southern voice made the question seem lyrical.

"Um, yes. I need a room. My friend, Kenna Mason, said she stayed here and that you might have a room available." Dani felt like a giant standing over this little old lady. She was close to six feet and this woman couldn't be over five.

"Friend?" She asked Dani. "Are you her then? Are you Danielle?" Her eagerness touched Dani.

"Yes, that's me. I was…" The woman launched herself at her and pulled Dani's head down into her pillowy breasts.

"Oh, my dear child! You poor thing! Oh, bless your heart! Everything you went through and how brave you've been hiding in New York City all by yourself. I'm so glad you came home to us." Dani's eyes started to tear up and even though she was virtually bent in half, she relaxed and fell into the woman's embrace. She was patting her back and stroking her hair and for the first time in four months, Dani felt safe and secure. No wonder Kenna had called the Rose sisters the fairy godmothers.

"I'm Lily Rae, now let's just get you inside and feed you, you must be starving. I already served breakfast, but I have a chocolate croissant left over if you'd like that."

"Thank you, Miss Lily. I'd love that." She understood the title of "Miss" now that Will and Kenna had used. She couldn't think of this sweet lady in any other way. "I'm Danielle De Luca, but everyone just calls me Dani. I'm wondering, though, how much this will cost me? I don't have any money right now. My account is still frozen, but I plan on getting a job."

"You think you can afford a hundred dollars a week?" Miss Lily asked as she led her up a grand staircase that curved upward to the second-floor parlor. She pointed to her left. "That was Kenna's room, but I've already rented it out for the week, so this will be your room." She opened the door to the right and Dani stopped.

"You sure you want just a hundred dollars a week? Are you sure it's not per night?" She glanced at the room trimmed in white lace. It was at least twice the size of her apartment in New York. The walls and the bedspread were a matching shade of pale yellow. A window seat overlooked the front yard and one wall featured built-in shelves. They were painted a bright white and housed a television and hundreds of books. She walked past the shelves and into the bathroom. Ah, heaven. There was a large vanity sink and a huge glass-enclosed walk-in shower. To be clean again! She had to stop herself from jumping in right then.

"I usually rent this room out for two hundred a night, but you're family, so you get the family rate." Miss Lily winked at her.

Dani turned and hugged her with all she had. "Thank you."

"Well, aren't you sweeter than honey? That's what friends are for, dear." She felt Miss Lily pat her back. "Now why don't you unpack and rest a bit. I'll bring up your breakfast in a jiffy." Miss Lily gave her one more pat on the back and closed the door on her way out.

Dani looked around the room and eyed the massive king-sized bed. She unpacked some of her things, but the draw of the shower was too much. She had been right; it was heaven.

She walked out of the bathroom and found a tray sitting on her bed with lemonade and a massive chocolate croissant. She felt a trickle of drool escape her mouth as she took a big bite. "Mmmm." She polished off the croissant while standing. After the last swallow of lemonade, her energy left her. She pulled her 9-mm Glock from her purse and put it in the drawer of her nightstand. She took the knife from the pocket of her shorts and placed it under the pillow. She stripped down and climbed into bed. As she snuggled into the cool, soft sheets, she decided the South wasn't so bad after all.

# Chapter Two

---

D ani dreamt of clouds. All she felt was the sensation of floating on a cloud. Until the cloud rear-ended another cloud and the cloud alarm went off. It took a while for her to realize the cloud was really her bed and the cloud alarm was her cell phone reminding her to go to lunch.

She forced her body out of bed, shaky with exhaustion. She only had a few clean clothes left, so it wasn't hard to decide what to wear. She picked out a white cotton skirt that swished around her knees and a bright red tank top with lace trim. She then slid her feet into one dollar flip-flops she got from Walmart.

Downstairs, Miss Lily bustled from one room to another serving food to the three guests. Dani waved and smiled at Miss Lily as she went out the door. She walked down the street but couldn't stop the feeling of paranoia. It had turned into a nice day. It was still hot, but a nice breeze had picked up. As she walked past people, they all looked her in the eye and smiled or gave a little wave. Feeling a little awkward, she gave a wave back. However, she couldn't help looking at each house, each person, and each car that passed by with a nervous eye. Her paranoia grew even worse when, for some strange reason, each car that passed by honked at her.

At the bottom of the hill, she turned left at one of the two stoplights in town. She looked at the small bank and shops that lined Main Street. She discovered the town had a calming effect on her.

The town could only be described as "quaint." She spotted Kenna standing outside the cafe, next to the windowsills full of white and pink flowers. She was talking to a pretty woman, a couple inches taller than Kenna with shoulder-length, light-brown hair. The woman was dressed in a short jean skirt and black stretchy top, but it was the belt that caught Dani's attention. It was bright pink, with green and white interwoven strands. It tied in the front with a perfect bow. She'd kill for that belt. She looked down at her white skirt and red top, both from Walmart, and sighed. Kenna and this girl were the fashion plates, not her. At least, not anymore.

Kenna saw her and waved. The pretty woman turned and waved, too. "Dani, this is my friend Paige. Paige, Dani."

Paige and Dani exchanged pleasantries and followed Kenna into the cafe.

She felt nervous. If she was honest with herself, she felt left out. Kenna had obviously moved on with her life. A fiancé, a new house, new friends, and fairy godmothers, she felt even more uncomfortable when they walked into the cafe and people stopped talking. She looked around and saw everyone turning to stare at her. It didn't qualify as paranoia when every person in the room was actually staring at her.

"Don't worry, they always do that with someone new," Paige leaned back and whispered as they made their way to a booth. They were about to sit down when two older women, one pleasantly plump and one resembling a beanpole, came racing forward.

"Is it true? Is Danielle finally home?" the beanpole with white hair asked as she came rushing past Kenna and Paige to wrap Dani up in a tight hug. What was it with tight hugs? They almost broke bones, but at the same time you couldn't help but wish for one.

"Move over, Daisy Mae." The matronly woman nudged the beanpole out of the way and grabbed Dani. Before she could ask who she was, Dani was bent in half and surrounded by soft, fluffy cleavage as the older woman stroked her hair and told her they'd look out for her. She tried to respond, but the words got lost in the woman's bosom.

She heard Kenna laugh and say, "Miss Violet, from experience I can say you might want to let her up for some air." Dani was released and the two women stood eagerly in front of her. Kenna stepped forward and placed a hand on the plump lady's arm. "Dani, this is Miss Violet Fae Rose." She patted the beanpole next. "And this is Miss Daisy Mae Rose. They own the Blossom Cafe."

"It's nice to meet you, ladies." Dani said. She still felt uncomfortable with everyone watching her and couldn't believe the lack of shame on their attempts to eavesdrop.

Kenna took the attention away from her and she could've hugged her for it. "Could we have some of that wonderful raspberry sweet tea and a round of chicken salad?"

"You betcha. I also just took out some fresh bread pudding and just made a new batch of bourbon butter sauce. Bless your heart, you must be starving. You're nothing but skin and bones. I'll bring some out for dessert," Miss Violet said as she hustled back to the kitchen and Miss Daisy took off floating from table to table spreading the news of her arrival to town.

She felt like the prodigal son returning home, but this wasn't home. It seemed to be Kenna's new home, but Dani didn't have a permanent home. She spent the last five years in New York City. While growing up, she split her time in Italy, Maine, and New York City. This was a state she had never stepped foot in. How could these people expect her to call this home? She closed her eyes briefly and decided they could think whatever they wanted.

Food and drinks arrived as quickly as the people started showing up at the table.

"So good you've come to our little town," someone named Pam Gilbert told her.

"Nothing like another pretty lady to liven things up," John Wolfe said with a wink.

Finally the people stopped introducing themselves and Dani felt like she could eat. The more she thought about it, the more she realized this wasn't just a Southern thing. And it wasn't as odd as she had first thought. She remembered the little bar in Milo, Maine, that served as the gathering spot for the locals and realized they would've done the same thing if a friend of her family came in. She thought of the outdoor cafe and wine shop her parents owned in Rivoli, Italy, and realized they, too, knew their customers and would recognize someone new with a regular.

"So the reason I asked you to lunch," Kenna started before taking another sip of her sweet tea, "was that I wanted to see if you were interested in working for me while we settle things in New York."

Dani had already asked for a refill and was heading for glass number three. It was amazing. She didn't even know she liked sweet tea! Dani thought about Kenna's offer. She was fighting conflicting feelings toward Kenna, but it wouldn't hurt to have a little money to spend. If things in Paige's shop were as cute as the belt she had on, then she knew she'd need it. She also wanted to make sure she could pay Miss Lily. She could always get money from her trust as it wasn't frozen, with the trustee in charge of each withdrawal. But she was determined to live on her own and away from her parents' fortune until she was thirty. She had three more years to go.

She had put herself through school on her own with scholarships from beauty pageants and modeling gigs. She bought and paid for that ugly brown Chevy Lumina all on her own. It was her symbol of independence. The terms of her trust fund stated that she could withdraw the money through her trustee, a manager at the bank. But she had to provide her parents with a detailed list of what she used the money for until the age of twenty-five.

She gained access to her trust at eighteen, but in typical teenage rebellion, swore to herself and her parents that she was an adult and not accountable to anyone but herself. In another fit of Teenage-Know-It-All Syndrome, she told everyone at the lawyer's office she wouldn't touch the trust until she was old. At eighteen years of age, thirty seemed old enough and she swore to everyone there she wouldn't touch it before her thirtieth birthday.

There had been some very hard times, scary roommates, lots of car trouble, and horrible jobs. In the end, Dani had reached the age of twenty-seven without touching her fortune. In all truth, only Kenna knew about it and for that reason she knew Kenna was giving her the opportunity to do what she loved while allowing her to stay true to herself and not touch the trust.

"That sounds wonderful. What do I get to do and when do I start?"

"Oh good! I was missing you in the office too much! You can start tomorrow if you want. You'll be doing a lot more client interviews and coming to court with me as well."

Dani was starting to feel alive again. Even if it didn't quite feel like the home everyone thought it should be, it was definitely nice. And if the bread pudding with bourbon butter sauce was any indication of the desserts here, she was in heaven. No fifteen-dollar skimpy serving of artsy food here!

"If you want, we can head over to the office now. You can meet the secretary, Tammy, and the attorney who owns the building, Henry."

Paige gave a snort.

"What?" Dani asked.

"I think it's more fun if it's a surprise," Paige said as she nudged Kenna. They burst out into giggles. Just as quickly as the feeling of inclusion came, it left.

Paige said goodbye at the moss green building housing the Henry Rooney Law Office and the McKenna Mason Law Firm.

"Come on in. I'd say welcome to your new home, but no more ninety-hour work weeks for us! Welcome to your office that you'll use mostly during regular business hours." Kenna opened the door and Dani was met by a nice lobby with a brown leather couch and accented with its own pixie.

"Dani, this is Tammy. Tammy, this is Danielle, my paralegal from New York." Tammy came out from behind her desk and they shook hands.

Dani was pretty sure she had just met Tinkerbell. The woman's hair was short and spiky. It was dyed more yellow than blond. She was tiny in every way. She couldn't weigh more than one hundred pounds and she'd be shocked if Tink was five feet tall.

"Oh! Kenna's friend from New York. I'm so glad you made it down. Did you run into any trouble?"

"No. Besides my car constantly overheating, there were no problems. It's nice to meet you."

"We're going to have so much fun working together! Yell if you need anything," Tammy said as she raced back to her desk to answer the phone.

Kenna walked Dani through an archway and into a hallway lined with offices. A man about her height and just a couple of years older sat on a leather couch reading the latest law updates. He looked up and his eyes stopped on Kenna's breasts and never quite made it to her face. When Dani came to stand beside Kenna, she noticed his eyes move up only so much as to account for the height difference between Kenna's breasts and hers.

"Hey, who's your friend?" His courtroom slick voice annoyed her already.

"This is my friend and paralegal from New York, Danielle De Luca." Kenna turned back to her. "Dani, this is Henry Rooney. And no, his eyes haven't made it up to your face yet."

Henry stood and Dani noticed he had an amazing ability to avert his gaze to any body part besides the face. She was also sure he had so much gel in his hair that she could see her reflection.

"Do you happen to have a band-aid?" Finally he moved his eyes to hers. He wasn't bad-looking, rather handsome really. His nose was a little large for his face and his tan a little too orange, but he had a great smile that made his brown eyes dance.

She shook her head. "No, sorry I don't."

He walked toward her, his eyes somehow deepening in color. His lips pouted slightly. "That's too bad. I think I hurt myself when I fell for you. You think you can kiss it and make it better?"

The laughter hit so strong and quick she doubled over. Tears rolling down her cheeks, she grabbed for Kenna only to find her leaning against the door with her head thrown back and hand on her hip trying to catch her breath. She took a gasp of air and tried to stop laughing. She and Kenna were still giggling a minute later.

"Oh, I haven't laughed in four months. Thanks, Henry." She put her hand on his arm as she stifled some giggles trying to escape.

This prompted him to overcome the shock of being laughed at to return to his normal, sleazy self again as he slid his hand over hers. "Anything else you haven't done in four months that I can help you with?" His gaze had dropped to her breasts again.

"You need to be neutered," Dani laughed as she removed his hand from hers and took her own hand off of his arm. He had sexual harassment written all over him, but it was more amusing than dangerous. He was kind of like a big puppy dog that just wanted to be loved but tended to hump your leg to get your attention.

"Well, at least I got you to laugh." Henry shrugged and turned back into lawyer mode. "So, you want to take the middle office?" He pointed to the second office of three down the hall. The third was Kenna's.

Kenna straightened up and Dani recognized her negotiation stance. "How much do you want for that other office?" Kenna inquired.

"Actually, I was thinking of a trade. If Danielle is alright with answering phones and covering for Tammy when she goes to lunch or is on vacation, I wouldn't charge you rent."

Both Henry and Kenna turned to her. "Is that okay with you, Dani?" Kenna asked.

"Works for me." She shook Henry's hand to seal the deal and pulled it back after he held on a little too long and offered her a wink.

# Chapter Three

D ani walked down the street and looked into the store windows as she headed back to the bed and breakfast. The stores lining Main Street were filled with antiques, local artwork, and a fresh market filled with local produce. She climbed the stairs at Miss Lily's and plopped down on the porch swing. It had been calling her name since she checked in that morning. She laid down on it, sinking into the soft chenille fabric. She left one foot hanging slightly over the edge so she could push off on the ground and slowly swing.

She was trying to relax, trying to prepare herself for tonight. She was dreading the interrogation by this FBI agent. Over the last four months, she developed a hard time trusting anyone. Police officers, FBI agents, private security… they all lied about what happened, who was where, and what they wanted done to her and Kenna. Trusting this FBI officer tonight was doubtful. She took a deep breath and tried to calm her queasy stomach. Her nerves were definitely getting the better of her. She heard the front door open and close.

"This was Kenna's favorite spot, too. She loved it so much she had Will hang one on their back porch." Miss Lily sat down in the closest chair and set a large pitcher down on the small table between them. Miss Lily reached over and gently took Dani's hand when she sat up. "What's the matter, dear? You're so wound up I thought you'd snap. I can tell by your eyes that you've seen more and handled more than someone your age ought to. But you can relax now. You're among friends."

Dani wished that was true, but she knew her enemies wouldn't rest until they had her and Kenna.

"Here, this will help you relax." Miss Lily poured a glass of what looked to be iced tea and handed it to her.

Dani took a sip and sputtered.

"That's my famous sweet tea with bourbon. Thought you could use an extra kick to help you relax a little." Miss Lily paused and her eyes widened as an idea hit her. "I know what you need! You need a man."

This time Dani choked. "Miss Lily!" She coughed a little before taking another sip. The stuff was good and after four months of having no alcohol, she was already feeling that tingling feeling wash over her.

"That's exactly what you need. Someone to share your burden. Someone to share some other things with, too," Miss Lily giggled, taking a sip of her own tea. "I know the perfect person, well, persons. Kenna's friend, Paige, has five brothers! One is too young, but there are four eligible bachelors for your picking."

Dani gave a little snort before taking another drink. "I'm sure Paige would love to have me as a sister-in-law. You think she'll help hook me up?" she said sarcastically.

"Sure. Although it's kinda hard to choose between my brothers," Paige walked around the side of the house and up the stairs to take a seat on the porch.

Dani felt her face turn red and decided to bury it in her spiked sweat tea. Great. With Paige's arrival, Dani was once again the third wheel.

"I thought Miles would be good. No, wait! Marshall would be best. After all, he owns a security company." Miss Lily clapped her hands together and nodded to herself as if it was a done deal.

"When Kenna had some of her trouble, I tried to have Agent Parker bring Marshall in to help. But nooo, Mr. Big Shot FBI Agent thinks he can do everything himself." Paige turned to Miss Lily. "You think I can have a glass of your special brew?"

"Sure thing. I'll be back in a jiffy."

Dani was pretty sure Paige felt just as uncomfortable as she did. She didn't know what to talk to her about and it was sorta weird sitting next to her replacement. "So, what kind of problems has Kenna been having? I thought everything was picture-perfect here until Chad found out where she was. Kenna never mentioned anything except that she was fine."

"It seems Kenna left a lot out. I'm sure it was nothing compared to what you went through, but she was hospitalized after Chad tried to run her down with a truck out at Will's farm. She only got away when Will hit the truck with a couple of rounds from his rifle."

"I didn't know. Was she hurt badly?"

"She was unconscious for two hours and bruised pretty badly down one side. Then Whitney attacked her at the Derby in a horse barn," Paige explained.

"Who's Whitney?"

"She's Will's ex-wife. But more importantly, she's Senator Bruce's daughter. Whitney Amber Bruce."

"I've heard both names before." Dani closed her eyes and saw the men in cheap black suits walking in front of her. They were talking about the senator and Whitney, but she hadn't known the connection until now.

"I'm pretty sure they're both evil. After Whitney spilled the beans about Chad's attempted murder and everything she knew, Kenna thought she was going to be safe. She sent for you and waited for you to get here. That's when she got a package from Chad. It was a picture of you and her with Chad in the middle, taken on the night of her birthday. He told her he'd never forget you two. It freaked her out pretty badly. She's put on a pretty good face, but she's been affected. She's one of the strongest people I've ever met. Now that she has her mind set on bringing them down, she isn't quite as afraid."

Miss Lily opened the door and brought out a new pitcher of sweet tea and an extra glass for Paige. "So, have we decided on Marshall then, or one of the others?"

Dani stared out the window of Paige's pick-up truck as they made their way to Kenna's house for the debriefing. Maybe she had been a little too fast to judge Paige and Kenna. Paige told her about her family of five brothers and her love of the outdoors. She learned that Paige had started Southern Charms all on her own and wasn't the simpering Southern belle she had assumed her to be. She was starting to realize her first impressions of everything in Keeneston were wrong. As she and Paige talked and shared stories about growing up in the country, she felt some of her bitterness wash away.

They pulled into the driveway and parked next to the standard government-issued black Ford Explorer. Dani looked over at Paige when she groaned.

"I can't stand him. I knew he was going to be here tonight, but he just drives me crazy."

"Who does?"

"Agent Cole Parker. He just, it's just that he's, I don't know. We just don't see eye to eye."

"Should I trust him then? I know people in the FBI are involved. Could he be one of them?" She closed the car door she had just opened and turned to Paige.

"No, it's not that. He's been a wonderful agent. He's working with higher-ups he personally knows and trusts to keep the whole investigation off the record. I can't explain it; we're just oil and water. Come on, I see him getting out of the car so I better introduce you two." Paige opened the door and walked around to Dani's side of the car.

Dani opened the door and stood waiting for Agent Parker to finish his phone call before introducing herself. It was hard not to notice Agent Parker. He had silver eyes under jet-black hair that was cut short, but not so short you couldn't run some through your fingers. All combined with a nose that looked to have been broken before gave off the most alluring appeal.

Paige moved around the car to stand next to Dani, waiting for Agent Parker to finish talking. Dani saw Agent Parker's eyes immediately go to Paige. Hmm, interesting.

He said something into his phone and then hung up. "Don't you think that skirt is a little too short?"

Dani was startled a little and then tried not to laugh. He was so serious and was posturing like a father of a teenager. She felt Paige stiffen next to her and put her hands on her hips.

"You're right about a problem with the length. Thank you for pointing it out," Paige rolled the waistband of her jean skirt one more time, hiding the cute ribbon belt and raising the skirt another inch up her toned thighs. With that move, Paige turned to Dani. "Dani, Agent Asshole. Agent Asshole, Danielle De Luca."

The second Paige had raised her skirt Agent Parker's teeth had clenched. She didn't know it was possible for him to bite his teeth together any harder than he already had until she watched Paige sashay right past them and climb the brick stairs to head inside. Agent Parker watched every step Paige took until the front door closed behind her.

He cleared his throat and finally turned to look at Dani. "Sorry about that. She's just so… Anyway, I'm Agent Cole Parker. I'm really interested in hearing what you have to say tonight. I hope you can give me a different angle to work things. My team and I always seem to be one step behind Chad and I'd love to turn the tables."

"I hope I'll be of some help, Agent Parker."

"Cole. We all work so closely together we've dropped all titles. Come on, let's head in. I think we're gathering on the back porch."

Dani stepped out of the house and onto a porch painted white. She saw over-stuffed chairs and a loveseat covered in blue-and-white striped material. There were potted plants on each side of the door and along the wooden railing. Pinks, reds, and purples all bloomed and seemed to fit right in with the natural green of the fields and trees surrounding the house. She took a seat on the back porch swing that was indeed the same one that Miss Lily had. Kenna brought out a variety of drinks, some cheese and crackers, and then sat down next to Dani.

"So do you want me to start now? Maybe it would be easier if you asked me questions, Cole."

"Hold on, Dani, we need to wait for Mo and Ahmed," Kenna said as she filled a glass with lemonade.

"Who are they?"

"Mo owns the farm next to ours and Ahmed is his security guy. They've been a big help during this whole thing. Ahmed is the one who got Whitney to talk. Ah, here they are now."

Dani looked to the side of the house to where two men were walking toward them. One man was of average height, maybe five ten. He was thick and had a cold look in his eyes that made her shiver. The second man made her shiver for a whole different reason. The second man was taller. Closer to six-feet or six-one and so smoothly handsome she felt as if she'd awakened from a four-month sleep. His features were sharp and clean. Amber eyes showed intelligence and a self-confidence that stopped short of arrogance. His dark hair was slicked back with minimal gel and stopped at his collar. Both men had lightly browned skin and features she placed as Middle Eastern or Mediterranean heritage.

"What's going on, dear? Did we have a breakthrough in the investigation?" his silky voice asked as he looked from Kenna to Cole. Dani saw his eyes then come to rest on her. She could tell he was trying to figure out who she was but was too polite to ask.

"Mo, Ahmed, I'd like to introduce you to my best friend, Danielle De Luca. Dani, this is Mohtadi Ali Rahman, or just Mo to his friends. And this is his head of security, Ahmed." Kenna smiled as she moved to sit back down after pouring the drinks.

"It's nice to meet you both." Dani felt her hands start to sweat and placed them on her knees, hoping the men wouldn't want to shake it. When she looked up from her lap, she saw that Mo was still looking at her. A blush crawled up her cheeks. She felt the intensity of his gaze all the way to her toes.

Ahmed cleared his throat and sat down next to Cole. She felt more than saw Mo take the seat next to her, but what she did see were Paige's raised eyebrows and Kenna's smile.

"Okay, Danielle, now that we're all here, why don't you tell us everything you remember starting with Kenna's birthday party." Cole pulled out a digital recorder and also a pad and paper.

With a nod, Danielle focused on the rolling green hills that made up Kenna's backyard and transported herself back to that night.

# Chapter Four

*Four Months Ago...*

The valet at New York's hottest club, The Zone, opened her door as she climbed out of Kenna's to-die-for car. At times, she felt bad that she always bummed rides off Kenna, but a hundred-thousand-dollar car should be worshiped. And boy oh boy, did she worship Kenna's cherry-red M6.

Kenna waved to the bouncer and Dani noticed she got the standard checkout. She rolled her eyes when the bouncer watched them walk past the velvet rope. It irritated her when men were so obvious. She knew because of her height she stood out and it embarrassed her when people would stare.

Growing up, she was the tall and lanky one everyone made fun of. In Italy, they called her *sottile alberello d'oliva*, or "the skinny little olive tree" in English. When she had moved to Maine, they had just called her Olive Oyl. She had been stick-thin, with no curves, no boobs, and no ass until she was seventeen. Finally, miracle of all miracles, her cup size grew from an *A* to a *C*. Granted, it was a small *C*, but a *C* nonetheless. She developed muscles from the skiing and hiking she enjoyed year round and built confidence from training on her rifle and bow. Even at twenty-seven years old with her gorgeous looks, she still felt like *sottile alberello d'oliva* on the inside.

She followed Kenna into the darkly lit club and let the thumping of dance music stir her blood. She loved to dance and couldn't wait to get out on the floor. She waved at the people from the office who had already hit the floor or bar. She and Kenna made their way to the back booth. A handsome, preppie man stood up from the table and kissed Kenna. He looked back at her and smiled. A cold chill traveled down her spine. Something about that smile scared her.

"Hey, pretty lady. Can I get you a drink?"

Dani turned toward the voice and looked down. A man, no more than five-six with his collar popped and his hair gelled in a tangled mess stood checking her out.

"No thanks. I'm here with my friend tonight." She knew she was a snob, but she couldn't date or even dance with men shorter than she. When she tried, she felt as if she were Gulliver visiting the Lilliputians.

The man walked off to find someone else while Kenna brought another man over to her. "Dani, this is Chad. Chad, this is my best friend, Danielle."

She smiled and he shook her hand. Some co-workers approached to wish Kenna a happy birthday, but Chad still didn't let go of her hand. "It's so nice to meet you. Kenna has told me so much about you that I feel as if I know you intimately." He squeezed her hand just a little too hard and she felt the bones crunch together. He let go so fast she thought it must have been an accident. She couldn't let it go though. The smile, the way he said the word *intimately*, the prolonged handshake…something was off.

"Thanks. I heard a lot about you, too." She kept her hand behind her and started looking around for an escape. She wished the popped-collar guy would come back. Chad's white teeth blinded her, making her feel like Little Red Riding Hood being eyed by the Big Bad Wolf.

"Is this your first time to this club?" he asked.

"Yes. The music seems good and there are plenty of people to keep the dance floor packed." She again wished someone would come ask her to dance, but with Chad standing so close, everyone probably assumed he was with her.

"It's mine, too. I don't go to that many clubs. Never seem to have the time. How about I get you a drink?" He looked over to the bartender and raised his chin in slight acknowledgment.

"No thanks. I'm going to wait for Kenna." She looked at Kenna talking to some other attorneys and wished she'd hurry up.

Chad turned and took a step to Kenna's side. "Hey, babe, you're neglecting me. I want to get you a birthday drink and then a picture with my two girls."

"Sure! Dani! You have to be in the picture. Come on, let's go to the bar and get this party started." Kenna grabbed her hand and hurried her to the bar. "Two sparkling peach martinis, please."

Dani felt Chad approach and felt him standing so near to her, his front was touching her back. He leaned over her and placed his shoulder between her and Kenna. "Three shots of Grey Goose first, please. To celebrate my girl's birthday!" The bartender placed the drinks on the bar. "Thanks, man." Chad placed a twenty on the counter and passed out the shots, then signaled the bartender again, "Hey, man. Do me a favor and take a picture of me and my two girls?"

She had to lean past Chad to joke with Kenna about how hot the bartender was. "Well, at least you know he can actually get you a drink!" They both cracked up at the ongoing joke that out of all the offers to buy her a drink, hardly any man actually got to. They toasted Kenna and then took the shot while the bartender took a picture.

"Here you go." The bartender handed the phone back to Chad.

"Thanks, Dave." Chad took Kenna's arm in one hand and escorted her back to their table. Dani walked up to the bar and sat down on a stool. She looked at the hot bartender while he was waiting on other people. No nametag. She looked around the bar and didn't see a nameplate, chalkboard greeting, or any other decoration showing the bartender's name. Chad said he hadn't been here before, right? Oh well. She shrugged it off and waved down the bartender who may or may not be Dave.

Dave was easy-going. He stood about the same height as Dani and had brown hair and a goatee. He was wearing dress slacks with a Zone t-shirt. He was very muscled and looked like the guys who lived at the gym. She decided she'd let him buy her a drink. They talked a little and found out they went to the same community college. He did, in fact, work out a lot at FitNow, a gym that opened a couple of years ago with floor-to-ceiling front windows to inspire those walking by to join and to allow people like Dave to work out.

She put her empty glass down on the bar, waved bye to Dave, and went in search of Kenna. She found Kenna and Chad at the VIP table. Kenna had just finished her sparking peach martini that she loved so much.

"The birthday girl can't have an empty drink!" Kenna laughed as she lifted her empty martini glass.

She saw Chad check his phone and then say something to Kenna. Kenna's lower lip came out into a pout that quickly vanished into a look of annoyance. Maybe she wasn't the only one who found Chad a little too much. Chad gave her a kiss and rubbed his hand up Kenna's leg to… Hello!

"See you later, gorgeous," Chad whispered as he walked past Dani toward the door.

Dani ignored the icky feeling she got from him and went to sit down by Kenna who promptly decided it was time to dance.

Two hours later, Dani rummaged around her purse as Kenna drove back to the office to pick up a file she had left behind. She was relieved when Kenna had admitted she was going to break up with Chad.

"Dammit! I must've left my keys in my desk. I'll just come up with you." She zipped her purse closed and looked out at the city lights. Kenna pulled into her reserved spot near the elevator and they went up to their floor.

"That's strange. I thought I turned the lights off." Dani looked around at the brightly lit lobby and shrugged. She noticed none of the hallway lights were on and chalked it up to forgetfulness in her excitement to go party. Dani crossed the marble floor and headed toward her desk.

"I'll go look for my file. I'll meet you back here in a couple of minutes," Kenna said as she took off toward her office. She turned around the dark corner and disappeared from Dani's sight.

Pulling out her chair, Dani sat down at her desk and opened her top drawer. She rummaged around and pulled out the paperclip box and felt the weight of her keys hidden inside. She pulled them out and placed them on the table. She tapped her foot waiting for Kenna and looked at her stylish heels and sighed. They were sexy alright and could heat up the dance floor but did nothing for the drive home. Her car had decided it would only blow warm air for ten minutes before turning icy cold. As a result, it never got much warmer than forty degrees in her car.

She bent over and looked under her desk for her warm Uggs. Pulling them out, she slipped them on. She listened for Kenna but didn't hear anything. Kenna was famous for the mess she had on her desk, so she wouldn't be surprised if it took a while to find the folder she was looking for. Deciding she still had a couple of minutes, she went to the bathroom and searched the supply closet for a plastic bag to put her shoes in and sat back down at her desk.

Okay, it had been long enough. She decided to help Kenna look for the blasted thing. She got up and put on her coat. She slipped her bags on over her shoulder and palmed her car keys. Walking around the corner, she saw that Kenna's office was still dark.

"Kenna, where are you? You ready to leave yet?" She yelled down the dark hallway as she walked toward the conference room. She heard a whoosh of air and then a sound like someone hitting something. Before she could investigate, she saw Kenna appear at the end of the hallway running toward her.

As she got closer, she saw blood running down her mouth. Her shirt was torn across the front and left hanging open. Her skirt was shoved up around her waist.

"Kenna, what the fu…"

"Run!" Kenna screamed as she grabbed her arm in a full run, causing Dani to spin around.

"What happened to you? Kenna, stop! Tell me what happened!"

"Kenna!" Dani turned toward the name being bellowed from down the hall and gasped at the sight of Chad with blood trickling down his face and clutching his balls. It didn't take but a second to figure out what happened.

They took off in a dead run for the stairs. She could hear Chad's labored breathing and heavy footsteps on the thick carpet as he raced after them.

"We gotta haul ass, girl!" Danielle said as she flung open the door to the stairs.

"You have to be careful. He's dangerous and so is Bob. I'll explain when we get out of here. Just get to your car and get home. I'll call you," Kenna huffed as they flew down the stairs heading to the underground garage.

Dani raced down the cold cement stairs and thanked God she had switched to her Uggs. She reached the heavy fire door first and ran through it. She went to the left as Kenna sprinted right to her car. Luckily, she had nabbed the first spot this morning, so she only had a short distance up the ramp to her car and reached it before Kenna reached her own car. With the keys already in her hand, she jumped into her car and prayed it would start on the first try.

The engine roared to life and she headed down the ramp. She saw Chad standing behind Kenna's car and didn't know if Kenna would have the guts to hit him. She decided to take the choice away from her and floored her Chevy. Surprised, Chad turned as she narrowed her eyes and pressed harder on the gas pedal. She had known right from the start he was an asshole.

He didn't have time to jump out of the way. When he turned to look at her speeding toward him, she plowed into him. He bounced off her hood with a surprised look in his cold eyes. She couldn't help but smile as she honked her horn in communication with Kenna. As she sped away, she looked to see where he landed but couldn't find him. Hopefully, she killed him, but scum like that was hard to get rid of.

Twenty minutes later, she crept up the dark stairs heading toward her small efficiency apartment. Slowly, she made it to the fifth floor and stood outside her apartment with her ear to the door. She knew from her very active neighbor that you could hear any noise through the walls. Listening for a couple of minutes and only hearing her ice dispenser, she unlocked the door and went in. She threw the deadbolt and plopped on the red plaid couch she had taken from her Mom's old room at the resort in Maine.

Sagging a couple of inches into the sofa, she laid her head against the back cushion. What had just happened? She didn't know if she'd ever get over seeing Kenna running to her with her clothes ripped and bleeding from her lip. What was even worse was the look on Chad's face when he came running after them. She had been frozen in place at the sight of Kenna, but the look on Chad's face was enough to send her running. His cold, calculating eyes would be enough to elicit fear in any sane person. However, it was his twisted smile, more like a sneer, that really freaked her out. The smile told Dani that he was enjoying the torment and fear he saw in them.

She nearly screamed when her phone rang. She looked at the caller ID and answered immediately. "What the hell is going on?" she asked Kenna.

"Danielle, listen, we don't have much time. There was this stripper and Chad was going to rape her in front of all the VIP's, including Bob. They were cheering him on. They were going to go next. I couldn't just stand there and do nothing. I called 9-1-1, there should be a tape. I barged in and tried to stop it, but Bob just dragged this young girl out of the room. It was horrible. Anyway, Bob sent Chad after me while those bastards dragged the girl out the other door. Chad knocked me around, but with your interruption, didn't get a chance to do anything else."

"Shit. I mean, shit, Kenna! What are we going to do?" Danielle stood up and started pacing her small apartment.

"Bob just called here. We both threatened each other. We gotta get out of here, and I mean now. I'm packing right now. Withdraw cash, toss your firm's cell phone, and get out of town, Danielle. You have my private email, and I know no one else has it. Email me on that when you get a new address so we know how we're doing. Keep it vague until we know what's happening here."

Danielle grabbed her black book out of the top kitchen drawer that contained Kenna's personal email. "Okay girl. You stay safe and I'll get in touch with you. I'll pack up and leave within the next twenty minutes. Legal Sisters?" she sighed. It was the nickname some of the associates called them since they were always together.

"Always," she heard Kenna say before the line went dead.

"Oh my God. What has happened?" She moaned as she fell back against the old refrigerator. Her phone rang again. She stood up and in one step was across the room and looking at the unknown number on the caller ID. That single moment changed her forever. She knew it when it happened. As the phone continued to ring, she knew it was bad and she knew it would get worse. She also knew she had two options. Run and hide, or stay and track.

Her Grandfather Darin, on her mom's side, had taught her everything there was to hunting and tracking. While she didn't like killing animals, she did enjoy the thrill of the hunt and the challenge of finding the animals. By the time she was sixteen, she'd spend a week roaming the wild forests of Maine around her grandfather's resort. While she took her rifle with her for protection, the main hardware she brought was her camera. She had loved tracking different animals and taking photos of them in their natural habitat.

Her grandfather had taught her the tracking skills, but it was her mother who had taught her how to blend into nature.

That thought was enough to make up her mind. She wouldn't run. She'd blend in and find out what the hell was going on.

Danielle stretched and pulled the 9-mm Glock from under her pillow. She had allowed herself three hours of sleep after she had packed. In the early morning hours, she had carried garbage bag after garbage bag of her clothes, keepsakes, and other belongings down the five flights of stairs and out to her car.

Her furniture would have to stay, but she planned to leave it there for the landlord in lieu of rent payment. The landlord wouldn't care and she was sure some of it would end up in his first-floor apartment.

The hours she had spent packing and climbing one painful step after the next gave her time to formulate a plan. She had called hospitals and found Chad had been admitted for a broken nose, stitches to his eyebrow, and a fractured leg. Posing as his primary physician in D.C., Dani discovered he was out of commission for at least four weeks while the leg healed.

At least she didn't need to worry about him coming after her. What she did have to worry about was the private investigators the law firm had on retainer. They were sophisticated and as mean as sewer rats. Most importantly, they didn't care what side of the law they fell on, as long as they got paid their outrageous fees.

She pulled on her jeans and a black sweatshirt. Tying her long dark hair into a ponytail, she slipped her feet into the Uggs and calculated the time it would be in Italy. It was five in the morning in New York, so it would be eleven in the morning in Italy. Her parents would be getting lunch ready and seeing to customers. Looking around her bare apartment, she spotted the firm's cell phone by the microwave. She picked it up and dialed her parent's number at the winery.

"*Ciao,*" her mother's American-accented voice said in Italian.

"*Ciao, Mama.*" Danielle smiled as she heard her mom yell for her father to pick up the extension.

"*Buon giorno, mia bella figlia,*" her father's deep voice came on over the phone.

"*Buon giorno, Papa.*" She was fighting back tears thinking this could be the last time she talked to them. Shaking her head, Dani clenched her hand into a fist and reminded herself to stay positive. "I'm sorry I can't talk long." She looked at the clock on the microwave and recorded the time she placed the call in an old spiral notebook she had found while packing. "I'm meeting Kenna and we're going on a trip to some spa for a couple of days."

"You'll miss work for this spa?" her father asked in heavily accented English.

"Yes. It's a reward of sorts. Kenna just settled a big case and gave us this spa trip as a thank you. I just wanted to tell you so you didn't worry when you couldn't get in touch with me. I'll give you a call when I get back."

"Oh, I am so jealous. Have a great time, dear. We love you." Her mother was always so kind and gentle. You'd never know talking to her that she was such a competitor and expert on survival skills for the wilderness. Skills Dani was already adapting for the city.

"Thanks, Mama. Love you and Papa. I'll talk to you soon." After hanging up, she recorded the time. It had taken three minutes to place the call and talk to her parents. She shoved the spiral notebook along with pens, pencils, markers, and an old digital camera into an oversized bag and headed down the rusted-out fire escape.

She slung the bag over her shoulder as she stared down at the ground, one story below her. Stupid fire escapes. Why couldn't they ever go all the way to the ground? She took off her gloves and shoved them into her back jean pocket. She quickly swung a leg over the rusted red rail and bent to grab the lowest rung. She slowly moved her feet off the edge of the fire escape and felt the cold of the rail bite into her hands when all her weight was transferred. She dangled off the escape and looked down. She was only about five feet off the ground now. She took a deep breath and let it out. Then she let go of the rail. As soon as she hit the ground, she rolled to reduce the impact. She stopped and listened to the sound of her impact echoing off the surrounding brick buildings. When she didn't hear any footsteps running toward her or windows opening to see what was going on, she stood up and dug her gloves out of her back pocket.

Rummaging around her bag, she pulled out a pair of fake black-rimmed glasses all the athletes wore. She put them on and pulled out a mirror and black eyeliner. She drew bigger eyebrows and gave herself moles on her face. The simple changes, along with hiding her hair under a knit toboggan, made her appearance much more masculine. If they had a picture of her, she might be able to walk by them and not be noticed. They might look but would then dismiss. Blending in, she thought, is the goal of a good tracker.

Dani started the long trek at a quick clip. She had parked her car six blocks away. She circled around to her car and pulled out a basketball. She didn't look around as she bent over to tie her shoe on the car next to her. Slipping out a screwdriver from her sleeve, she unscrewed the license plate of the Toyota Prius parked next to her. She let out a breath when she didn't hear anyone scream at her.

It was still dark at five-fifteen in the morning. The street was quiet, and only her footfalls made any noise on the empty street. But lights were starting to come on in apartments and she had to be cautious when a jogger would come by on his morning workout. Luckily, it was the weekend so people tended to stay inside longer. She slipped her plate from her bag and quickly screwed it onto the Prius. Pretending to look for something in her bag, she slowly walked to the back of her car and quickly attached the stolen plate to her car.

Making sure the car was locked and the keys were easily accessible, she ran back toward the front of her building. She approached from the far side of the street and looked at her watch. Five-twenty-five. She felt it before she could register what it meant— the tingling that ran along her body. She always got that feeling when she was on the trail of an animal she desperately wanted to photograph. She looked again at her building and noticed the lights being turned on in her apartment. Sliding into a doorway across the street, she hid in the darkness and pulled out her notebook.

She noted the time her light went on and then off. The best she could figure was that they arrived within twenty minutes. That was a pretty broad area that they could've come from, but it told her they weren't local. The front door to her building was flung open and three men dressed in black came out. They stood next to the black Mercedes parked in front of the building.

Digging out her binoculars, Dani wrote down the plate number as the rear window was rolled down.

"We didn't find her." Dani strained to hear the conversation.

"What do you mean you didn't find her? Where could she have gone at five in the morning?" She recognized Chad's voice instantly.

"We listened to the recording device we left in the apartment. She talked to Kenna. She knows what's going on but doesn't know who was involved. Then she talked to her parents at five and told them she and Kenna were going away together to a spa," explained one of the muscled men in black she recognized as a firm investigator.

"So they're together. Figures. If we find Danielle, we'll find Kenna. Focus on getting to Danielle now. She's some beauty queen, so it won't be hard to find her. It's not like she's all that smart. What kind of brains does it take to wave at people? She'll leave a trail."

Danielle smiled. She loved being underestimated.

"You want us to get the bug?" another muscleman asked Chad.

"No, leave it. Then we'll know if she comes back. Make sure to put a flag on any calls going to her parents' house from the U.S. and freeze her accounts. She doesn't have money like Kenna does. She'll be forced to come out sooner if she needs money."

Crap. She pulled out her wallet and found seven dollars. She had forgotten about the money. She watched as the men piled into the car and took off down the street. She turned and sprinted three blocks down and over two to the nearest ATM. She pulled out the limit from each of her three credit cards, which was three hundred dollars. She then cleaned out the two hundred in her checking account. She was trying to pull her money out of the savings account when the screen popped up telling Dani to see a representative.

She looked down at the cash in her hand and was somewhat relieved she was able to get eleven hundred out before they froze her accounts. She walked the remaining block and a half to her car and noticed the Prius was gone. She checked her plate and saw the stolen one was still attached. No one ever remembers their license plate numbers. She smiled at her minor victory as she got into the car and pulled out a city map. She estimated how many miles she could travel in fifteen minutes and drew a circle around her apartment. It was a lot of ground to cover, but it was a start.

On a gut feeling, she drove toward Greendale, Thomson & Hitchem, or GTH for short. Copying the move at her apartment, she parked a good distance away. Still within a distance easily covered in a five-minute run. She grabbed the basketball again and walked in the early morning light toward GTH. She felt her confidence bolster in the early morning light. There was something about walking through a city like New York in those hours. It was quiet. She felt like she was a conqueror. The only noise being the soles of her feet hitting the pavement. A basketball court frequented by the younger executives during lunch was a block down the street from GTH. She opened the gate and went in. She could watch from her position, but she wouldn't be able to hear anything.

An hour later, she was sweaty and tired of playing basketball by herself. She had to leave her bag in the car since she was hoping to pass as a man. She slumped and slid down the chain link fence to rest. She opened her notebook and started to doodle. Traffic had picked up and she kept her eyes glued to the parking garage entrance as she doodled. A black Crown Victoria pulled up and parked in front of the building. A short man in his early thirties got out and reached back into the car. When he stood up, she watched him clip a gun to his hip and put on a navy blue windbreaker with FBI across the back.

She had to suppress a laugh as she watched him check himself out in the car's window reflection. What a peacock. He seemed much more impressed with himself than anything else going on around him. He'd be the weak link. If someone was so focused on how important he was, then he tended not to pay attention to anything he considered beneath him.

As soon as he deemed himself presentable, the FBI agent went straight into the front of the fancy glass building flashing his badge at the front desk security. This time, Dani did laugh out loud as she gathered her things and headed to get her car.

"Crap. Where is it?" Dani rummaged around her makeup kit looking for her smut gear as she liked to call it. "Ah-ha!" She pulled out long dangly earrings along with some bright pink eye shadow. She put on the earrings and applied heavy makeup. The more she caked it on, the more she looked like someone else. She turned around in her seat and dug around for the costume bag she remembered to pack. She silently thanked God for all the Halloween parties she went to. She felt around and came out with a blonde Farrah Fawcett wig. Still turned around in the car and pulled out a suit coat and some heels. Dani struggled to take off her Uggs and put on some heels. She stripped off her sweatshirt and put on the suit coat. It wrapped around her waist and tied at the side, letting her wear it without a shirt underneath. Her lace bra would be visible if she moved certain ways, which was exactly what she wanted.

As she put on her wig, the FBI agent walked back out of the GTH building and got into his car. She put down her mascara and turned her car on. She followed him into the section of town that hosted the courthouse along with various governmental branch offices. He pulled into a garage across the street from the FBI building and walked into the office.

Dani gave him a minute and then got out of the car and hurried toward the building. On the inside she was shaking, but on the outside she portrayed a rushed assistant. "Just breathe, just breathe," she kept repeating until she got to the front door. Ripping open the door, she rushed to the man at the information/security desk.

Here we go! Putting a hand on her heaving chest she smiled and in her best Jersey accent said, "Oh my god! I was supposed to get that agent's name for my boss and I forgot it! Can you believe that? He told me and then it just went right out of my head. My boss wants to call him and," she paused to take a deep breath, "this is just so embarrassing, but I misplaced the card he gave me." She leaned over the tall desk and didn't try to close her jacket when her breasts started playing peek-a-boo with the guard.

She smiled sweetly when his eyes moved to her breasts and froze. "Um," the guard cleared his throat and finally brought his eyes up to her face. She batted her lashes and the guard continued. "You don't remember any part of his name?"

Running her tongue nervously over her lips, she waited until he was distracted again. "He just came in here. He's about five-six or - seven. Dark hair that is slightly thinning, and not at all handsomely like yours is. He's trying to cover it up and it looks funny." She jutted her breasts out again as she ran a finger over the guard's thinning hair he had cut extra short.

"That would be Mark Edwards. He's on the eleventh floor in Public Corruption. Do you need his number?" the guard rasped out.

"Ohh, that would be great!" she pitched her voice and laughed, knowing he'd only be looking at her jiggling breasts as he handed over the information. "Thank you so much, you saved my job. Not to mention a horribly embarrassing situation. Have a good day!" She swung her hips as she walked out of the door. Hopefully, if anyone ever asked about the woman who came in, all he'd be able to say is that she was blonde, from Jersey, and had great tits.

# Chapter Five

*Three months ago…*

One week after her visit to the FBI building, Dani opened her wallet to see how much money she had left. She had spent fifty dollars on food and two hundred on a week-to-week roach motel. She'd have to shell out another two hundred today if she wanted to stay. After having to spend another fifty dollars in gas, she only had eight hundred left.

"Okay, Dani, one more week in the cheap hotel, but no more McDonald's. No more coffee. Just free water and beef jerky for a while." She went down to the hotel's front desk and paid for another week and then went back to watching Agent Edwards.

She had called all the hospitals, morgues, and escort services she could find in the past week looking for the girl who was attacked by Chad. So far, she had turned up nothing. She had tried to get a copy of Kenna's 9-1-1 tape, but there was mysteriously no record of it. The responsible party was either the firm's investigators or Agent Edwards. She pulled out a big blanket and put it over her legs. Her car's heater didn't really work all that well to begin with. But the need to save money prevented her from letting the car idle.

"Thank God!" She nearly yelled when she saw Agent Edwards leave the building and head to his car. She followed him to a NYPD station and watched him go inside. So, maybe it was Edwards who made the tape disappear. He left thirty minutes later. Dani waited a while before she walked over to the nearest payphone and called the NYPD.

"Hello? This is Stephanie London at GTH. FBI Special Agent Mark Edwards was supposed to come in and file a report today. Could you tell me if he did that?" She took out her pad and pencil when she was placed on hold.

"Ma'am," a cold, snooty woman's voice came on the line, "what exactly are you calling about?" Dani could hear the suspicion and knew the call would be traced in a split second if she didn't act quickly.

"Ma'am, as I told the person who answered, Agent Edwards was just in there filing a report. I'm an attorney with GTH and since we're involved with this delicate issue, we wanted to know what the report stated. Agent Edwards was supposed to send us a copy for our records, but when I just talked to him he said he forgot to get me a copy. So, please, I need the name, date, and time the report was filed. I need it for a motion that must be filed in court today!" She let out an irritated breath to stress urgency to the person on the other end of the line. She then held her breath as she could tell the woman was debating on what to tell her.

Finally, she heard some keys clicking on a keyboard. "He filed the Material Witness Affidavit for McKenna Mason and Danielle De Luca at eleven fifty-three. Judge Dick LeMaster signed the Material Witness Order at twelve-oh-six."

Whoa. That was fast. He must have signed the information needed and then had a courier hand-deliver it to the courthouse down the block. She looked at her watch; it was only twelve-fifteen.

"We put out an APB on both cars at twelve-eleven. We have a note here to call Agent Edwards with any information that comes in on the case."

"Thank you so much. I can finish my motion now." She hung up and sagged against the payphone. There was an APB out on her car. Good thing she changed plates. She looked down at the pad and knew the risk was worth it. She had just gotten another name, Judge Dick LeMaster. The only way that order would be signed so fast is if LeMaster was involved with Agent Edwards and GTH.

The next three days were far less productive. She learned nothing from following Agent Edwards. She decided to leave the car at the hotel and walk around town some to think. Her thoughts kept coming back to the men in black, as she liked to call them. Whom did they work for? Each time she saw them, Chad and an investigator from GTH were there. But she didn't know the other men. Maybe it was time to learn more about them. She walked into the center of town and swiped her Metro card. Dressed as a man again, she carried a gym bag and basketball into the subway. She took a seat on the train and waited to see what, if anything, happened. At the next stop, three men in black got on the train. One was the firm investigator. Dani sat bobbing her head as if listening to music and watched as they walked by. She glanced at them as they made their way down the train. Any woman with dark hair received a tap on the shoulder and a stare-down. Dani tried not to show her relief. It was clear they didn't know what she looked like aside from height and hair color.

The tight knot in her stomach relaxed slightly. When the train stopped, the two unknown men in black got out. Yet the investigator remained on the train. Harnessing her courage, Dani strolled out with her basketball under her arm and her big black glasses perched on her nose. The hood of her sweatshirt was negligently tossed over her tobogganed head and she had sagged her pants, looking like a regular street baller to anyone who might have noticed.

She followed the men up the stairs and onto Eighth Avenue. They turned around and she willed herself not to stop in her tracks. She stared ahead of them and kept her pace slow and steady.

"It's just some kid," she heard one of them say.

"She has to be around here somewhere. She didn't get off when we got on. Either she got off here or she's still on the train."

"I still don't understand what the senator wants with her, do you?"

"No, but who cares. He told us to get this bitch, so we will."

"What have they found out about the other one?"

"They haven't looked. Figured this one would be easier to find."

The first man grunted. "Doesn't appear to be so."

"That's why the senator is getting so mad. She's been spotted so many times, yet we can't catch her. Come on, let's circle back around and see if we can find her." They turned down a side street and Dani kept walking.

"Dammit to hell and back," she said under her breath. Police were looking for her, an FBI agent was involved, a judge, and now a senator.

Two nights later, she lay in her lumpy bed at the roach motel and stared at the map. She had narrowed the men in black to an office near a building that housed the New York State Congressmen when they were home. The senator involved was either Bruce or Tamlin, but there was no way for her to tell which one.

Her rent was almost up and she couldn't decide if she should stay here for one more week. Her funds were getting dangerously low. Since the awesome roach hotel didn't have any curtains, she cursed when cars came into the parking lot lighting her room up as if it were midday. When the third car pulled up, she got curious and looked out the window.

"Shit!" She jumped down from the wobbly chair and tugged on a pair of jeans. She grabbed her cosmetic bag, costume kit, and an empty bag. She ran to the miniscule bathroom and scooped as much into the empty bag as she could. She managed to snag a sweatshirt with a hood, her Uggs, and another pair of jeans before opening the back window and jumping out. She heard the crack of the flimsy front door as she ran between buildings heading for her car parked four blocks away. Thank goodness she didn't park it in the lot. She had lost a bag of clothes, but at least the men in black hadn't gotten her, yet.

She heard the shouts notifying the others that she had gone out the back and pressed herself harder. She heard more shouts ordering the men to spread out. Their heavy feet hit the pavement hard as they ran after her. Sprinting as fast as she could, Dani took giant gulps of air as her lungs started to burn. She slammed into her car and yanked open the door. She tossed her stuff into the passenger seat and prayed the car would start. She jabbed the key into the ignition and turned. Nothing. "Come on! Come on!" She turned the key again and her Chevy roared to life. She slammed her foot on the pedal and took off as fast as she could.

Dani woke up on a cot at Saint Mary's Shelter with the feeling of being watched. She looked around and saw a little girl no older than two staring at her. She smiled and tried to see what time it was. She gave up on going back to sleep and got up to use the bathroom. When she came back, a man was asleep in her cot. Deciding it wasn't worth the hassle of trying to get the cot back, she headed out to find her car. It had been one month since the incident and so far she hadn't learned anything concrete. She had no idea how the men in black found her last night, but it made her real jumpy.

She got into her car and headed to the nearest public library. She tried closing her eyes again, but the fear of being chased kept her constantly looking around. After the first rush of people walked into the library, she went inside and jumped onto the public computer. She stared at the free email sign-up trying to think of the best name to use. Smiling to herself, she signed in as a client of Kenna's, a sweet old man by the name of Mr. Fox. She sent her message updating Kenna and logged off. She didn't waste any time hanging around and went back to her car.

The second month in New York was spent in a constant state of dread. She laid low at homeless shelters and in her car. She had less than five hundred dollars left and was about to give up. She had followed Judge LeMaster for two weeks and followed Agent Edwards for another week. She spent one week trying to tail Senator Tamlin, but could never stick with him. His driver was amazing, and Dani was too scared to push it.

She opened her second spiral notebook and dated the page April 28th. She shifted in her seat and got comfortable before taking notes. She was down the street from the senators' offices. Next up, she was going to try her hand at tracking Senator Bruce. She opened her window and let the cool breeze come in to wake her up. She noted what time Senator Tamlin arrived and was relieved to see Senator Bruce pull in shortly after. Both were in town to campaign for some bill they were sponsoring.

Thirty minutes after they arrived, another car pulled up and parked in the adjacent parking lot. Dani shot forward and then immediately hid behind her steering wheel as she recognized Chad. Her heart literally stopped and she felt her fight-or-flight mode kick in. Part of her wanted to hide and cry, while the other part of her wanted to reach for her 9-mm and shoot the bastard.

Chad sauntered into the building and left an hour later. She hit the wheel in frustration as both senators left within five minutes of each other. There was no telling which one Chad went to see. She followed Bruce and watched him give a speech in Central Park about the environment and the importance of green space. She didn't spot Chad again, but just seeing him once was enough to freak her out and make her realize she needed to stay. If the judicial system, the police, the FBI, and now a congressman were all working together, then she had no one to turn to for help. She was the only one left to find out what happened to the girl and gather enough evidence to bring down this whole circle of corruption.

"*Ciao*, Mama." Danielle slipped another quarter into the payphone.

"*Bella!* We've tried calling, but your cell phone goes straight to voicemail. We were so worried that we almost came looking for you." She heard the relief in her mother's voice and felt horrible for not calling her parents sooner.

"I know, I lost the phone at the spa and then we got this huge case. We've been working nonstop for the past month. It looks like we'll be at trial in a couple of weeks, so my schedule is insane. I just wanted to let you know that I am okay. I haven't gotten around to replacing my phone either. I'll do that soon and call you with the new number."

"Are you eating? Are you getting enough sleep? It's not healthy to work so hard."

"Yes, Mama. I'm fine. Hold on." She put her hand over the receiver and pushed away the tears falling from her eyes. She wanted to be in the safe embrace of her parents so badly. "Ma, that was Kenna. We have to go. There was an emergency hearing called before the judge! I'll talk to you soon. Love you and tell Papa I love him, too."

She waited to hear her mother tell her she loved her too and then hung up. She walked into the building behind the payphone and changed into her street baller gear before heading out the back door and circling around. Based on her location, the men in black would get to her within eight minutes. They made it in seven. She watched from the basketball court across the street as the regular three men in black got out, this time accompanied by Chad. The men looked over to the basketball court, but only saw the ten men playing on the court. They didn't see Danielle sitting in the stands with some others watching the game.

It had been three days since she'd seen Chad and she needed to know if he was still in town. She pulled out her notebook and wrote May 1st on top of the page and detailed the time and who showed up. They walked up and down the street and then came over to the court.

Chad walked onto the court as arrogantly as possible. Her stomach turned. He was only fifteen feet away from her. She took deep silent breaths to calm herself and acted alarmed as everyone else was, that someone had the audacity to interrupt the basketball game.

"What the fuck, man?" one of the players screamed as he stormed over to Chad.

Chad calmly took out his wallet and pulled out five hundred dollars and held it in the air.

"Whacha want, man?"

"I want to know if any of you've seen this woman?" He pulled out a picture of Dani from the birthday party. It was clearly taken when she wasn't looking and it disgusted her knowing Chad had probably taken it.

Everyone looked at it, including her. Some shook their head but one boy of about thirteen spoke up, "Yeah, I saw her on the payphone. She went into the building behind it."

Chad stripped off a hundred and handed it to the kid. "Did she come back out?"

"I don't know. I wasn't watching for her."

"Did anyone else see anything?" When he got no response, he turned back to the kid and gave him another hundred. He looked up, examining every person in the stands. Dani had to keep eye contact. Her heart was racing and she was surprised Chad couldn't hear it.

Before he could get to her, one of the men in black came jogging over from across the street and stopped next to Chad. "The woman at the front desk said Danielle came in through the front doors then went to the stairs. She hasn't come out the front door, but could've left through the basement."

"Shit. She's long gone then. I think it's time I went and paid Kenna another visit. This time I'll stick around to say hello." Chad's lips curled up into a twisted smile.

Dani's stomach rolled as if she had just been punched. Bile shot up her throat and she had to swallow it down. Trying not to show the anxiety building up she scribbled the conversation down in her notebook. The men gave one last look at everyone and turned to head back to the car.

Dani cheered and pretended interest in the now-resumed game until she was sure they had left. She walked out of the park and down the street to an internet cafe near where her car was parked. She ordered a water and sat at the only open computer.

*He's coming* was all she had time to write to Kenna before she saw the men in black. They were spread out and slowly walking both sides of the streets looking at the parked cars. Chad must have called for reinforcements. Dani pressed Send and logged out. She walked to the bathroom and hoped there would be a window. There was one, but it took several precious minutes to pry it open. She climbed out and ran through the back alleys to her car. She saw one man walking away from her across the street.

She slowly made it to her car door, keeping an eye on the man's back the whole time. She inserted her key and worried he'd be able to hear her unlock the car. She placed her hand on the door handle and slowly lifted it. She heard the loud pop of the latch coming free when she heard the shout. "Hey! You!" She looked up and saw the man in black dodging traffic and making his way toward her. She flung the door open, jumped in the car, and peeled away from the curb as the man reached for her door. She heard his scream and when she looked back in the rearview mirror, she saw the man jumping around on one foot. She smiled, her car may be a piece of shit, but it did a great job running over scum.

She floored the gas pedal, knowing the man was calling in her location to the rest of the team. She drove straight until the man was out of sight and then started zigzagging her way toward town. She drove to the FBI lot and pulled in the parking garage. No way would they think to look for her here. Looking down, she found that her hands were shaking. Her heart was beating so fast she was afraid she might have a heart attack. "Okay, girl. What now?" She pulled out her notebooks and started reading through them again.

# Chapter Six

*Two months ago...*

D ani stood off to the side of the ninth hole at the exclusive Overland Private Golf Resort holding Judge LeMaster's golf bag. She smiled as Judge LeMaster's putt went in. "Good job, sir," she complimented as she took his putter and placed it back into the bag.

It had been a month and a half since she hid in the FBI parking garage. After reading over her notes, she decided that Judge LeMaster might be the key figure. A sitting judge would have enough sway to send an FBI agent out on tasks, such as filling out an affidavit, more so than the other way around. She spent three weeks following Judge LeMaster and his family everywhere. She had learned what summer camps his kids were in, when his wife went to play tennis, and more importantly, when Judge LeMaster went to play golf every week.

She had pulled on a black button-down shirt and some khaki pants. She bound her breasts with an ace wrap and found a boy's wig. She gelled the hair and threw on some boy's shoes before heading to the golf course. She had written her name as Scott Tamlin. When the interviewer asked if there was any relation to the senator, she answered in a convincing teenage boy voice, "Dad doesn't like me to use his name to get things. I'm supposed to have a real job this summer and get it on my own. So don't say anything, please?" The woman happily nodded at the chance to provide a senator's kid with summer employment and gave him a job as caddy.

The woman in charge of HR for the club bugged her for a copy of her social security card, but so far Dani had managed to push off the issue. When she arrived at work that day, she discovered the HR department was undergoing transition and thanked her lucky stars. She knew she had just bought herself some more time.

She played ball, cards, and did just about anything else to be the caddy for Judge LeMaster's group and today she was finally assigned to him. It was a comfortably warm day for the middle of June, and the group was excited to be out on the links after taking a couple of rounds of drinks at the clubhouse. The group consisted of an Assistant Director in Charge at the New York FBI office, a U.S. federal judge, and the vice mayor of New York City. It was a very powerful group and Dani had learned more about corruption in the first nine holes that she could ever imagine.

She also learned the group of men had a thing for younger women who liked it rough. She had to hide the snorts of laughter that attempted to erupt when the four men talked about all the action they got. All of them were the perfect example of middle-aged men. Rounded bellies, thinning hair, and some even had gray hair. If they weren't paying for their action, she guessed most twenty-year-olds wouldn't even notice them.

"Hey, Gene, anything going on at the FBI we need to be aware of?" Judge LeMaster asked as he waited for Jarred Felting, the vice mayor, to finish his putt.

"I have Edwards keeping an eye on the GTH issue for you. I can't believe the incompetence of Bob's men. It's been four months now and all we know is that McKenna Mason is well protected in Kentucky." Gene Pottinger slashed a blade of grass with his putter. "Chad came into the office the other day to let me know some agents are asking questions about him. He can't figure out who and asked me to look into it."

"What's the game plan now? We're all going to be up shit creek without a paddle if one of those girls talks," Jarred said after sinking his shot.

The group turned and walked toward the next hole. Dani had to stop herself from running up to them and demanding to know more. Instead she kept her head down and trudged along behind them.

"I don't know about you, but I don't like how Chad is handling this. He needs to stop dicking around and take care of business, if you ask me," said Brian Voggel, the U.S. federal judge. The group murmured their agreement and teed up.

"I think the best plan is to let Bruce's men handle this. I just don't know if Chad can take care of those two women. Maybe we need to try something else," LeMaster whispered.

Dani continued to bob her head and move her lips as if she was listening to music. The men each looked around and relaxed when they saw the caddies seemingly entertained with each other or listening to music. "We'll talk about this more next week. Maybe Bruce or Chad will have something new to report. God knows Bob won't." Jarred shook his head and lined up his shot.

Dani sat in the caddie lounge and listened to her iPod. She glanced at the clock on the wall and prayed the caddies currently on the course moved slowly. There were only four of them in the room and any minute now, the judge's group would arrive. If they did, she'd be guaranteed a job.

The door opened and the head caddie came in. "Okay, I need you four." She jumped up and then made herself slow down. She pulled the earplugs out of her ears and slowly walked out of the room with the other three boys. This time, she was assigned Brian Voggel's bag and made a show of putting in her earphones and cranking up the volume so everyone could hear it. Every couple of minutes, she'd turn down the volume until it was eventually muted. Every time

Voggel came to grab a club, she'd un-mute it and he'd be met with blasting music.

On the thirteenth hole, the men looked around and signaled that they were all clear. There were no golf carts driving by, no other groups they were getting close to, and all the caddies were hanging back.

Gene Pottinger rubbed his mostly bald head and wiped his arm across his sweaty brow. "I have news." Dani stared off toward the lake on the right and bounced her head. "Chad's gone off the deep end. He thinks he's being followed and he thinks the FBI is investigating him. I've looked into it all, even the secret missions, and there's nothing. He swears he's being followed, yet when Edwards trailed him he didn't pick up a tail of any kind. On top of that, he was supposed to take care of that Mason woman and failed. He's too damn interested in playing games."

LeMaster took off his sunglasses and ran a hand down his face. "I don't like it. Tell Bruce to have his men watch Chad. I also think it's time to move forward with our plan. Tell the boys it's a go. I'm tired of sitting around waiting for the axe to fall."

Dani was surprised she could hear them over the beating of her heart. What did moving forward with their plan mean? She wished they'd talk more, but instead they quieted down when one of the other caddies come near to take Pottinger's club.

They finished up the game by talking about the new young things they were all sleeping with and didn't go back to the subject of Chad or GTH. The tone had been ominous, though. The boys were up to something.

That night Dani reclined the seat of her car as far as it would go and stared out the open window. She sat up and pulled out the map. Finding Kentucky, she worked to locate Keeneston. She had gotten an email from Kenna almost six weeks ago telling her where she was living and asking her to come. Kenna's theory was that they could face everything better together, even if the bastards knew where to look.

Dani didn't like the idea of letting them know where she was. But she was also getting really sick of living in the car. She was fairly well known at some of the shelters and had decided that living in the car was safer.

She found a tiny dot representing Keeneston outside of Lexington. Maybe Kenna had a point. It was now clear that the boys were going to try to get to Kenna and maybe she could help protect her. Of course, that put her in the line of fire too. But she'd been outwitting these guys for the past four months. She was confident that she could continue to do so, especially on neutral ground.

With her mind made up, she felt for her gun between the seat and the console and closed her eyes. Tomorrow she'd start the trip to Keeneston.

# Chapter Seven

Current Day...

Dani's eyes refocused on the group surrounding her. Cole was scribbling furiously in his notepad and everyone else was staring wide-eyed at her.

Kenna leaned over and wrapped her in a tight hug. "Don't you ever do something so stupid again!"

Dani tried to respond to her, but Kenna wouldn't loosen up her grip.

"That was a very brave thing you did, Miss De Luca." Ahmed gave a little bow of his head.

"You could have been hurt or killed. Someone such as yourself should never have to live out of your car. I am impressed by your survival skills but must admit very relieved you are now here," Mo said with a sigh.

Dani stopped breathing for a second when he placed his hand on her knee and gave it a squeeze. It felt like electricity was crackling between them. By the surprised look on Mo's face, she was pretty sure he had felt it, too.

Cole flipped to a new page and looked up to her. "You're positive the FBI agent was Mark Edwards? Short, thinning, dark-blond hair that looks like it's been styled to within an inch of its life?" When Danielle nodded, Cole glanced around to the group. "I went through the Academy with him. He was also stationed in D.C. with me. Was a real kiss-up, but never really got anything done. There was a rumor he had been transferred to New York on special request. I'll have to do some digging to see where that special request came from. If there was one, it would've to come from pretty high up the ladder." He focused on Dani again, his silver eyes narrowing. "I won't ask about your gun, but you may want to see the sheriff ASAP about getting a permit to carry concealed. Your New York permit won't transfer."

"I'll take her to get it," Kenna said. "I'll talk to Red and see if he can pull some strings and issue it immediately based on your New York one." Kenna laid her hand on Dani's shoulder, causing her to smile.

It was nice to have friends around. She was still trying to come to terms with how quickly this town had adopted her. No wonder Kenna liked it here. She leaned forward and looked at the group. "So, the real question is, what do we do now?"

"Well, I'll need to read over my notes. I have enough to pass on to my guys in New York. We'll see if they can track down the bartender and see if he'll lead us to Chad." Cole looked up from his notes. "That actually seems to be going well. I'm glad Chad is starting to feel the pressure. We can never seem to find him. We always arrive a minute too late. However, it seems our pressure and your efforts have put him at odds with his bosses. Luckily, my boss agreed to not even put this on the limited book. This investigation is only described on paper, locked in his private vault at the office. That's why Pottinger can't find anything on it." Cole shook his head and rested his chin on his hand. "This is huge. This investigation is going to rock the FBI, Congress, and the judicial system."

"I think your men need to start taping conversations between the golf buddies Dani told us about. Get some hard evidence to bring them down. It will also make them turn on each other once they know the ship is sinking," Ahmed said to Cole.

Cole nodded his head in agreement and scribbled some more notes down. "I also think we need to keep a close eye on the girls. I don't like the sound of whatever this new plan is. I have a feeling things are going to start moving very quickly. Dani, I have your taped statement, but I don't have Kenna's." Turning to Kenna, he continued, "Why don't we meet tomorrow and I'll get your official statement as well?"

"Okay. Sounds good."

"Then I think we need to look at that map of yours, Dani. Try to find the locations you think the men are coming from. We can start tailing them and hopefully they'll lead us to Chad. Top priority right now is to draw Chad out so we can arrest him." Cole stared at Ahmed with narrowed eyes. "Arrest, Ahmed."

Ahmed gave a barely visible nod of his head in response. What was that about? Dani turned to Kenna and raised an eyebrow.

"Ahmed would prefer to capture Chad and interrogate him," Kenna explained.

"I don't see the problem with that." Danielle looked at Ahmed and received a smile in return. Wow, she'd never seen a person whose face changed so much when he smiled.

"The problem is that when Ahmed finishes with Chad, he'd just disappear instead of being turned over to Cole. Thus making any evidence obtained inadmissible in court."

"Too bad. Maybe after his testimony he can disappear?" She looked at Ahmed and winked. She was rewarded with another smile.

Leaning over to Mo, Ahmed whispered, "I like this one."

Mo looked her in the eye and she felt butterflies take flight in her stomach. "I do, too," he said, never taking his eyes away from her.

"Well, I hate to break this meeting up, but I'm going to run out to see Miles before it gets too late." Paige stood up and stretched her arms above her head before grabbing her purse.

"Miles?" Cole asked quickly.

Dani noticed everyone turned to stare at him. She was obviously missing something. However, from the way Cole was checking out

Paige earlier by the truck, it seemed like there may be something between the two.

Noticing everyone was looking at him, he looked at everyone else. "What?"

Will cleared his throat and tried to contain his smile. "Nothing."

"It's none of your business who Miles is," Paige snapped back.

"Sure it is."

Dani saw Paige roll her eyes in response and head for the door. Cole turned and followed her out with a lecture on hanging out with strange men.

As soon as Paige and Cole were out of earshot, Will, Kenna, Mo, and Ahmed broke out into laughter.

"Would someone care to explain what just happened?" Dani asked.

Mo stopped laughing and stood up, a smile still lingering on his lips. "I could tell you all about it if you would allow me to escort you back to Miss Lily's."

She looked up to him as he held out his hand to her. Glancing down, she stared at his hands. They were slightly darker than hers and so obviously masculine in their shape and size. She reached out her hand and placed it in his. His hand was strong and warm. The heat spread slowly from her hand to her...ohmygod!

Dani quickly stood up and removed her hand from his. She wasn't quite sure if she wanted to throw herself at him or run as fast as she could in the other direction. Her body had never responded like that to a simple touch. "Thank you. I'd appreciate a lift." She said goodbye to Will and Kenna and started for the front door when she felt a warm gentle pressure on her lower back. She glanced to her side and saw Mo looking down at her. She couldn't help the small smile that came to her face as he guided her to the silver Mercedes.

She stood back and allowed him to open the door for her. She slid in and was slightly googly-eyed as she took in the interior of the car. She was used to Kenna's BMW M6 and used to think that was the most amazing car out there. But Mo's put the BMW to shame. Apparently there was good money in horse farms.

Mo slid into his seat and turned toward her. "Would you like to stop for dinner? I know it's late and we had some snacks, but I thought you may want something more filling." Mo's question triggered a loud rumble in Dani's stomach. "I'll take that as a yes. It's a little out of the way, but there is a great restaurant in Midway, which is about twenty-five minutes away." He started the car and headed out of town.

"So, tell me about your farm," Dani probed as she looked out at the winding country road. She saw lots of horses and cows dotting the countryside.

"It's about five hundred acres. I started it up last year and this is the first year I will have horses I have bred running and training on it. I brought some horses with me from my homeland of Rahmi and then bought a few from Will's farm. In a couple of years, I hope to have one of the best racing stables in the country."

"Sounds fascinating. I must admit it's all new to me. I grew up in Northern Italy around grapes and then moved to the wilderness of Maine when I was thirteen. I went to school in New York City, but spent most of my free time back in Maine. Neither place is known for horses. Actually, most animals in Maine were for hunting, not racing. I've never heard of Rahmi; tell me about it." She laid her head back against the seat and watched Mo confidently drive. He looked like he should be in a Gucci ad or sitting behind a massive desk on Wall Street, not raising horses out in the middle of Kentucky.

"Rahmi is a small island country near Dubai. The primary income is through oil production and fishing. I have a small racing stable there that raced in Dubai and England. However, I have always wanted to win the Kentucky Derby."

"Is your family still there? I know how hard it is to live so far away from them. Mine spend most of their time in Italy now." She looked down at her lap when she felt him put his hand on her knee and give a reaffirming squeeze. His hand looked good there, she thought. She looked up and saw him casting a questioning glance at her, as if asking permission to touch her. She felt his hand relax when she gave him a quick smile. She looked back out the window and tried not to focus on the sensations his hand was causing.

"My parents and my older brothers are in Rahmi, but my sisters moved away when they were married."

"Wow. That must have been nice having such a large family. Were you all close?"

"No. Sadly we were not. My father can be a bit dominating. Everyone had their roles. So we never got a chance to form bonds that come through child's play. I have made a promise to myself that when I have children of my own, they will not be held to such strict standards. They should be able to enjoy their childhood." Mo removed his hand from her leg as he pulled into a parking lot. "This is Midway. Lots of arts, crafts, antiques, and home-cooked food."

She glanced down one side of the circular street and then up the other. Apparently this was it. It couldn't be more than a quarter mile long, but she saw the warm glow of shop lights. People sat outside and numerous displays caught her attention, begging her to go shopping.

Mo got out of the car and opened her door for her. He extended his hand and she took it as she stood up.

"Here we go," he said as he pointed to one of the restaurants. Mo escorted her through the door and they were quickly seated at a small table for two. Dani was at war with her feelings as her knee brushed up against his. It was impossible to feel what she was feeling so soon. She had only known this man for hours, not months.

She spent the rest of dinner looking for a reason to squelch these feelings for Mo. By the time dinner was over, she was falling even deeper for him. She had hoped he was arrogant, but he never mentioned his money. She hoped he was egotistical, but he only talked about himself when she asked. She hoped he was boring, but he captivated her with his conversation. She hoped her interest in him would wane when conversation died down, but it never did. He kept her laughing with funny stories from the horse world and got her to talk about the amusing things that went on behind the scenes of beauty pageants.

"I guess we should be going. I think they want to close," Mo said and he glanced around the restaurant.

Danielle looked away from his face and couldn't believe the restaurant was empty. Well, damn, so much for squashing her fascination with Mo. All tonight did was cement these feelings. She was starting to understand what her mother meant when she said falling in love felt like being run over by a big logging truck.

Danielle felt the familiar sensation of Mo's hand on the small of her back as he escorted her up the walk to Miss Lily's front porch.

"Thank you for accompanying me to dinner tonight," Mo said as they stopped in front of the door.

"No, thank you. The food was wonderful and so was the company." She felt her face heat and laced her hands together in an attempt to calm her nerves. She was hopeful and fearful that he'd kiss her at the same time.

He moved in closer and placed his hands on either side of her waist. She felt him pull her in close. Oh my, he was going to do it. She closed her eyes and felt his lips above hers while his fingers squeezed into her hips. A bright porch light flipped on and the screen door banged open. They whipped their heads around and found Miss Lily, broom in hand, standing by the door. She could've sworn she heard Miss Lily mumbling something like, "Not another one."

Dani slipped on a t-shirt Miss Lily had washed for her that day. She unpacked the laptop Kenna loaned her and signed on. She pulled up Skype and called her parents via videophone. She stared at her picture in the box on the screen and startled. She had lost a lot of weight. Her face was almost hollow. No wonder Mo kept ordering desserts for her and why the Rose sisters kept sending over food. The darkened box on the screen came alive with picture of her mother and father's face.

"*Grazie a Dio!*" her father whispered, laying his cheek against her mother's head. "We thought you were dead!"

She watched as tears rolled down her mother's face. "What has happened, Papa? Why would I be dead?"

Her mother shot up from her seat. "What happened? I'll tell you what happened. We got a photo of you and some man, along with a copy of your obituary! And you ask us what happened?"

Her mother never screamed. Dani's imposing height, athletic frame, blonde hair loosely tied back, and piercing blue eyes were enough to make her skiing competitors shake in their boots. But her mother screaming was enough to make Dani very thankful she had never pissed her mom off before. However, she had never seen her mother this worked up before and it scared her. Her father, with his olive skin, same height, dark brown eyes, and black hair slightly salted, was the complete opposite of her mother. He was calm, quiet, and still whispering his thanks to as many saints he could think of.

"What photo, what obituary? I don't understand."

"Your boyfriend, Chad, sent us a picture of the two of you along with his condolences on our loss," her father explained. He picked up a picture and brought it to the camera. It was the picture from Kenna's birthday, but it had been cropped to show just her and Chad. "Daughter, I believe you have some explaining to do."

An hour later she had explained the situation to her parents. She had told them about Kenna, Chad, GTH, her time in New York, what she had learned, and her arrival in Keeneston. Her parents were ready to book plane tickets to arrive tomorrow, but Danielle assured them that the local FBI was on top of it. If her parents were here, she wouldn't be able to focus on catching Chad because she'd be too worried about him targeting them. They had agreed that they'd give her one month. They booked their tickets for July and told her if she didn't check in via video chat every day they'd be on a plane that night.

Dani logged off the computer and climbed into bed. She felt so much better being able to talk with her parents. Despite being an ocean apart, they were always close. Tonight she finally felt close to them again after four months of short conversations and leaving them in the dark. Her mother had given her advice on checking the area out and looking for hiding places or escape routes. Pulling up the covers and rolling onto her side, Dani slept for the first time in four months.

# Chapter Eight

Dani sat back in her chair and put down the highlighter. While Kenna was in court that morning, she had been doing some research on Chad. She compared the origin of the UPS package from Chad to the areas of town she had spotted him. She color-coded a map of the city and scanned it. She had just emailed it to Cole and Ahmed when the intercom rang. Tammy's voice told her Kenna was on the phone.

"Hey, girl."

"Hi, D. We just got out of court for the day. Can you join me at Blossom's?"

"Sure. I just sent some info to Cole and Ahmed, so I'm at a good stopping place. Be there in just a minute."

"See you in a few."

Ten minutes later, Dani walked down the street. Sweat trickled down her back and her red sleeveless silk shirt clung to her breasts and back. Jesus, it was hot. She looked up at the bank sign that displayed the temperature and was shocked when it read only eighty-eight degrees. She would've sworn it was at least a hundred.

"Good afternoon, Miss Danielle."

Dani looked up and saw John Wolfe in black dress pants and a sports jacket walking toward her without a single drop of sweat on him. He was magical. "Hi, John. Actually, you're the perfect person to ask. Is it always so hot?" She knew the answer couldn't be good when John just laughed.

"Honey, this ain't hot. Wait until August. This is just the humidity. You're not used to it yet. By the way, did you enjoy your dinner date last night?"

"How on earth… What they say about you is true, isn't it?" Dani asked. She and Mo had been in a completely different town. John just shrugged and took off down the street whistling.

Dani pushed open the front door and thought she'd faint from the joy of feeling air-conditioning. She took in a deep breath and all thoughts of being hot fled when she smelled the food. She spotted Kenna in the back booth and started toward her.

"Excuse me."

Dani turned and saw a cute girl a couple years younger than she dressed in scrubs. She was sitting at a table full of women in matching attire.

"Yes?" Dani took a quick glance at the back of her skirt to make sure she didn't tuck it in her underwear. Usually when some one stopped you politely, it was tell you your panties were showing or toilet paper was trailing after her.

"We were all wondering what dinner was like with Mohtadi." When the girl said his name, she added a little sigh. Oh my, Mo had girls fawning over him!

"How did you know Mo and I had dinner? And, I'm sorry, but who are you?" Dani felt Kenna step up next to her.

Leaning over, Kenna whispered, "Welcome to the Keeneston Grapevine." Kenna then gestured to the girl, "Dani, this is Amanda Webber. She and the rest of the ladies work out at Doc Truett's Large Animal Vet Clinic." Leaning back over to Dani, she whispered again. "You might as well tell them. Everyone will just keep asking until you tell them everything. It's really quite fascinating. And, I want to know, too!" She smiled.

Dani looked around the room and found that most everyone had put their forks down and angled their chairs to face her. When Kenna gave another little nod, she decided to give in. "Well, it was nice. We ate in Midway, which I'm guessing you all already knew."

The nodding heads confirmed her suspicions.

"But what is he like? He's so mysterious," Amanda said with a dreamy tone to her voice. The others at the table nodded their agreement.

"Um. He's great. He's friendly, polite, and funny. That's all I can really say," Dani shrugged.

"Are you going to see him again? Is The Bachelor off the list?"

"I have no idea if we'll go out on another date. But I do count him a friend. So I guess he's still on whatever list you want to put him on." After she signaled she was done with questions by turning toward Kenna, the conversation level rose to near-deafening. She heard lots of discussion about his qualities, or lack thereof.

Kenna slid into the booth first and as Dani was getting in, said, "You know, he's rather a mystery to most people. For the longest time, they thought he was the cause of all the problems at Will's farm. He has only recently started coming to town functions and letting people get to know him. That's why they are so curious."

Dani shrugged her shoulders and picked up the menu as Kenna continued talking.

"Actually, the reason I asked you here is because I have a secret to tell you."

This caught her attention. She put the menu down and placed her elbows on the table as she leaned forward to hear. Kenna dropped her voice and also leaned toward her. "The engagement party next week isn't really an engagement party."

"What in the world does that mean?"

"It's actually going to be my wedding day!"

"What!" Dani clamped a hand over her mouth when she realized she had spoken way too loud. She glanced around at the room and saw many people looking their way. "Sorry. You kinda took me by surprise there."

Kenna's smile looked like it couldn't be contained. "When you know it's right, it's just right. So, Will and I thought to surprise everyone. Well, that and we didn't want to wait any longer! Betsy has invited everyone we would have invited for the wedding anyway. I've talked to Judge Cooper and he's going to marry us. I want to know if you'll be my maid of honor." Kenna bit her lip as if she was worried what Dani may say.

"Girl, you're crazy if you think for one minute I wouldn't kill you myself if you asked anyone else!" Dani felt a real smile come over her. Her friend was truly happy and that made her happy in return.

"Great! I found my dress by accident when I was shopping the other week. I also found two amazing bridesmaid dresses. One in pale pink and one in pale green. I went ahead and bought them. I'm storing them at Paige's. She hasn't seen them either, so I was hoping we could run down there and surprise Paige. We can also try on the dresses to pick out which one you want."

"Screw lunch! Let's go now," Dani said as she looked around for Miss Daisy. She looked back to Kenna when she heard her laugh. "What?"

"I already ordered our lunch to go!"

Dani reached behind her back and zipped the dress. She felt the satin dress kiss her legs as she wiggled around to help the zipper up. The dress was pale pink and strapless. It had a fitted bodice with an A-line, tea-length skirt. It was so Kenna with the clean lines and classy appearance. She twirled around and couldn't help laughing like a little girl when the skirt billowed out.

She pushed open the curtain of one the changing rooms at Southern Charms and came out to find Paige similarly spinning in front of the three-sided mirror set up in the hat room of her store. Dani had been taken aback at first by the hat room. Hats filled the room from front to back. Paige had made small, large, and really freaking big hats in every color combination. She had never seen anything like it before. She looked away from the hats and checked out Paige's dress. Paige's dress was the exact same as Dani's but in a pale green color that matched her tanned skin tone perfectly.

"Kenna, these are great!" Dani exclaimed.

Paige nodded her agreement before doing another spin. The spinning was contagious and Dani couldn't help herself as she spun round and round.

"I stole this from the fridge at work." Kenna pulled out a bottle of champagne and Paige giggled again.

"I swear, I am not a big giggler. It's just this dress. It makes me feel like I'm seven years old and playing dress-up." Paige spun around one more time with her head thrown back, eyes closed and arms lifted outward.

Dani laughed and took the full champagne glass Kenna offered her, then Paige.

Kenna lifted her glass. "To old and new friends. I'm so glad you'll be there with me on my wedding day." Standing in a circle surrounded by her best friend and her new friend, Dani couldn't help but feel the first strands of contentment wash over her.

Two hours later Dani placed the dress in her office and sat down at her large oak desk. It was only three o'clock and she needed to get some practice on the new case law research program Kenna used. She logged on and started working the terms and connectors to find what worked best for specific areas of law.

She answered the phone when it rang and immediately regretted it. A woman was screeching at her children and didn't even hear Dani when she answered the phone.

"Hello?" Dani yelled into the phone.

"Yeah, I need to talk to a lawyer."

"I'm sorry, Ms. Mason is out of the office right now. Can I take a message?"

"You a lawyer?"

"No, ma'am. I am Ms. Mason's paralegal. I can set up an appointment if you'd like."

"Naw. I don't wanna pay for nuttin'. You'll do. Let me tell you what's going on."

That phrase brought fear into the even the most seasoned assistant. Sure enough, the lady started in with her story so fast that Dani couldn't interrupt.

"You see, my boyfriend moved into my house three years ago. We have four babies, ages seven, five, three, and six months, and now he's leaving us to starve all because of some ho. When we started datin', he hired me to work in his photocopy store as his assistant. Apparently, while I was at home giving birth to his son, he was out banging the temp on the copier. Found a picture in my desk with her claw-like nails diggin' in to his pasty ass. That bitch put it there for me to find. Of course, he fired me when I confronted him. So I did what any respectable woman would do. I drove my car into the shop and now I need a lawyer since they said I committed some kind of crime. That bastard deserved it. Besides, it was discrimination. He couldn't fire me because I was on maternity leave. I want to sue!"

Thirty minutes later, Dani hung up the phone. It was hard to make the woman understand that Kenna couldn't take those cases since she'd be the one prosecuting the case. On top of that, the woman was adamant she hadn't committed a crime and kept asking Dani why they'd throw a mama in jail when she was the one with the case against the boyfriend.

Danielle looked up when she heard the bell over the front door and heard Tammy direct the person to her office. A couple seconds later, Mo stopped at her door holding a bouquet of a dozen calla lilies in a beautiful crystal vase. Her heart sped up at the sight of him in the dove-gray suit. The flowers, the man, the suit… it was too much. She knew in that split second she was about to fall head-first into love with him.

"I am sorry to interrupt your work. I just wanted to drop these off and see how the dress worked." He placed the flowers on the corner of her desk and moved around to face her. He leaned over and placed a soft kiss on her cheek. "I also found myself unable to think of anything but you."

That did it. She was now face-first in the love puddle. "Thank you. I must admit I found myself thinking about you a lot, too." She looked into his amber eyes and was lost for a moment. "Wait. How do you know about the dress?"

Mo chuckled and picked up her hand. He brought it to his lips and turned it over, placing a soft kiss on the pulse point of her wrist. Heat shot up her arm and she found herself licking her lips, hoping that he'd move up her arm, over her shoulder, up her neck, and then nibble his way to her lips.

"Will and Kenna asked me to provide my private security team for the wedding. Speaking of the wedding, I was hoping you would do me the honor of escorting you."

"I'd love to." She felt just like she was in high school and had been asked to the prom. This was a day for happy feelings. She watched Mo move to the chair on the other side of her desk and take a seat. She was feeling some other very teenage emotions when she watched him walk away from her.

"How are you adjusting to living in Kentucky?" he asked when he sat down.

"Okay. The town is a lot like Milo, just a lot hotter and nosier."

"Milo?"

"Yes, Milo, Maine. That's where my mother is from. My grandfather runs a resort there. They have hiking, hunting, camping, fishing, skiing, and other sorts of things. I spent all of my breaks and every summer there from the time I was thirteen until I was out of college. My parents sent me to school in New York City, but we'd fly to Maine as often as we could. I think my mom missed the openness of the wild but wanted me to get a good education first."

"So you grew up in two completely different worlds?"

"More like three. I'd spend at least a month in Italy as well. And, of course, I spent the first thirteen years in Italy on my parent's winery." She loved having three vastly different places to go. She never felt closed in or bored. Her parents had made sure of that. "What about you? I'm sure Kentucky is even more of a culture shock for you."

"It was at first, yes. But, now I have grown to love it just as much as my country. The people are more open and freer with their thoughts. While I love my country, I love the opportunities this country provides."

"Are you going to make this your permanent home?" She felt that more was riding on this answer than even she understood. If he was planning on going back, she'd know the relationship was never going to advance past where it was now. The thought of that happening almost brought tears to her eyes.

"If I had my wish, I would stay here forever and only visit my country. I love this state and I love my horses. I am happy here. I wish to marry and have kids running around the farm."

Was it just her wishful thinking, or did he look right at her when talking about marriage and kids? The way her heart was jumping told her she sure hoped he did. "That sounds lovely. After spending time in so many different places, I've found that I long for the country again. I really missed the open air, fields of green, and trees not surrounded by concrete. The city was great when I was in college and for hitting the clubs, but not for a family. At least, not for mine." She felt her face flush and was slightly embarrassed to have shared such intimate feelings with Mo. It wasn't like he had asked her to marry him, but it felt like they were talking about a life with each other.

"Well, I should let you get back to work. Would you care to have dinner with me tonight? I could pick you up after work?"

She had to hide her grin. She loved that he blushed and got nervous asking her out, despite his normal confidence and natural swagger. "I'd love to. How about picking me up at six?"

"Perfect." Mo rose and walked back around the desk. "Just like you." He placed his hands on the arms of her chair and slowly leaned forward. Her eyes fell closed just before his lips met hers. His kiss was soft and sweet, almost a little unsure. She ran her tongue over his bottom lip and suddenly he seemed very sure. His kiss deepened and his tongue swept into her mouth. She felt a moan escape and melted into his kiss.

"Wow." Dani jerked her head back and looked toward the door when she heard someone speak. Tammy stood there holding a package and trying to hold up her jaw. "Can you teach me how to kiss like that?"

Dani laughed when Tammy batted her eyelashes at Mo. Catching onto the joke, he chuckled, too.

"Sorry, you're too young." He turned back to Dani and placed a quick kiss on her lips. "I'll see you tonight." Mo gave Tammy a wink on his way past her.

Dani could only nod as he left.

Tammy let out a wistful sigh and plopped herself down in the chair across from Dani. "Man, you and Kenna have all the luck. Kenna and Will, you and Mo... I've lived here twenty-one years and have never had a kiss like that from anyone."

Dani smiled. It seemed like a lifetime ago she was twenty-one instead of just six years. "Let me tell you a secret." She paused until Tammy looked at her. "No one has ever kissed me like that before and I had to wait twenty-seven years for it."

"Fine. I guess he's all yours. He may be smokin'-hot, but he's a little old for me anyway." Tammy stood up and walked back to her desk.

Dani shook her head and tried not to laugh at the conversation but couldn't help it. She turned back to her computer and started working again.

"Shoot! I'm so sorry, Dani." She looked up from her computer and saw Tammy standing in front of her with the same package in her hand that she had thirty minutes ago.

"Sorry about what?"

"This was delivered for you and when we started talking about hot guys and kissing, I kinda forgot to give it to you. That was the whole reason I had come back here in the first place."

"It's okay. No big deal. Thanks for bringing it back to me." She looked around her desk for something sharp as Tammy walked out.

Not finding any scissors, Dani used her car key to rip open the tape. Who would send her a package? It was probably something for the wedding from Kenna. She pulled open the top and saw an ivory card lying on top. As she picked it up, she felt the earth give way underneath her. It felt as if her stomach was free falling and white noise filled her head.

*Here's a toast for your new job. I got you something for your desk. Be seeing my two girls real soon. Maybe we'll make it a party of four?*

With a shaky hand, she put the card on the desk and looked into the box. She took a deep breath as she pulled out the framed photo of her, Paige, and Kenna toasting with champagne just a couple hours ago. The realization of what that meant hit her along with anger. She had just found a place to feel safe, a place to start over, and that bastard wanted to play with her. She bounced the frame in her hand a couple of times before she threw it as hard as she could against the wall. The metal frame lodged into the wall.

# Chapter Nine

"What the heck was that noise?" Henry walked into her office and stopped. No smart-ass comments came forth when he saw her ashen face or the tears silently falling down her face. "Dani, what happened?"

"That son of a bitch." She tried to stop the tears from falling, but they still came even after she used the back of her hand to wipe them away. For four months, she lived in fear. She was tired of it. She was tired of running. She was tired of letting one night ruin the rest of her life. She saw Henry reach for the card on the desk.

"Tammy! Call the sheriff and get Kenna over here. Now!" Henry walked over to the wall and looked at the picture. "Nice dress. Really shows off your rack."

Dani's head snapped up and the shock caused by his comment stopped her crying. Then she laughed. Laughed so hard tears started to fall again. Henry was the greatest womanizer in the world. He had made her laugh when she thought she might never be able to again.

Henry sheepishly came over to her and gave her a hug. "So God does answer prayers."

Drying her eyes, she pulled her head back from his shoulder and looked at him. "What prayers?"

"I asked God for an angel to hold in my arms, and here you are." Henry ran his hand down her back and ever so gently cupped her bottom.

Dani didn't have the heart to hit him, so she found herself with her head on his shoulder, his hand on her ass, and tears spilling onto his shirt. She alternated between crying out of anger and laughter.

"Jesus, Henry. You're assaulting the poor girl." Dani lifted her head and saw the first man who welcomed her to Keeneston.

"Sheriff, it's nice to see you again." Dani stood up and swatted Henry's hand away. "I seem to have a bit of a problem."

"You can file sexual harassment charges if you'd like." The gruff old sheriff pulled out a small pad of paper and went searching for a pen.

"No. It's not Henry. It's this." She picked up the note and handed it to him.

"I'll call Agent Parker. He'll want to see this immediately. Was there anything else?"

"Yes, the picture." She pointed to the frame jutting out of the wall.

Red gave a soft chuckle as he looked at it. "Good arm, young lady. You play softball, because Saint Frances could use you in our summer league. Those Protestants kill us every year in the city playoffs."

Before Dani could respond, the bell over the door rang and she heard Kenna shout her name. "Dani! What happened? Are you okay?"

Dani pointed to the note and the picture. It killed her to watch the happiness from today drain away as Kenna read the note. When she looked at the picture, Dani saw her body start to shake.

Kenna turned around and looked Dani right in the eye. "You know what this means?"

"He was right outside our door this afternoon and we didn't even know."

Kenna nodded and they both sat down. The bell rang again.

"Who now?" Dani groaned.

"What happened? I heard sirens." Paige rushed into the room and looked around.

"Chad sent us a message." Kenna pointed to the picture and note on the desk.

"I called Will as soon as I saw Red stop his car out front," Paige said.

"Thanks, Paige."

"Oh shit. I'm in this picture. This was taken just a couple of hours ago. How could that be?"

Kenna and Dani both shrugged. Dani felt totally exhausted. From the looks of it, Kenna did, too. She didn't want to think about it. She didn't want to analyze it. Now that the adrenalin had worn off, all she wanted to do was sleep. Then she'd think about it. Then she'd come up with a plan for revenge.

Dani closed her eyes and listened to the noise of Henry, Tammy, Paige, and Red. She felt Kenna grab her hand and squeeze. She squeezed back. She'd just close her eyes for a minute.

"Kenna!"

"Danielle!"

Dani shot up in her chair and saw Kenna's arm slip and her head fall to the side before shooting upright.

"What?" They said at the same time.

Dani turned her head in her seat and wiped her face to help wake up. Apparently she and Kenna took a little catnap while debate raged over what to do next. A frantic-looking Will and Mo ran into the room. Tired of explaining, she just pointed to the note on her desk and the frame in the wall.

She saw both men clench their jaw and look at each other. Uh-oh, Chad was going to be in trouble. They both looked so fierce that Dani was almost afraid. But when Mo turned to her, there was nothing but kindness and concern in his eyes. Oh yeah, she was in love alright.

"About damn time you got here," Paige walked over to the door where Cole was standing. "We called you almost thirty minutes ago."

"I was in a meeting. Sorry it took so long. The local office got a call from Gene Pottinger, Assistant Director in Charge of the New York Office."

That got everyone's attention.

"Apparently we have two material witnesses in the area and our assistance is needed to bring them in."

"You wouldn't dare, Parker." Will moved to stand between Cole and Kenna. She noticed Mo shift to her side as well.

"Of course not. I told them we'd keep our eye out for them and let them know if anything turns up. The meeting I called was to make sure the other agents knew that Pottinger had asked me to do this. If they hear anything, they should let me know. I'll report that nothing has popped up on our radar. Now, Dani, why don't you tell me what happened."

"I got a package. I opened it and found that note." She pointed to the note. She noticed that the shock had worn off. She was no longer shaking or crying as she retold what happened. "Then I got a little mad and threw the photo he sent. It's there." She pointed to the wall. She really did have a good arm.

"Son of a bitch. Paige, you're in this photo, too, and he refers to you in the note. When was this taken?"

"About four hours ago," Paige answered. "But I want to know what you're going to do about all of this. We have the FBI trying to take them away from us and we have a psychotic rapist playing with them. What are you doing? Nothing, that's what!"

Dani sat back and watched Paige in a full rant. It was really something to behold.

"You walk around like some big shot when you can't get anything done. You haven't found this bastard. You haven't made them safe. Now because you can't get anything done, I'm in this sicko's sights." Paige threw up her hands. She pulled her cell phone from the back pocket of her jeans and punched in a number. "Hey. I need you. Something has happened. Yes. I'm at Kenna's law office. Okay. Bye."

"Just what in the hell was that all about?"

Paige got right into Cole's face. "I'm calling someone who I know can help." She turned on her heel and walked out of the office.

"What do you mean by that?" Cole yelled after her.

Kenna leaned over to Dani. "It's like a real live soap opera."

Dani grinned. She'd been thinking the same thing.


For the next ten minutes, Dani, Kenna, Will, Mo, Henry, Tammy, and Red took the opportunity to enjoy the Paige and Cole show.

"I bet they don't even know they both are completely crazy about each other." Kenna said.

"Nope. Just like me and my Susie were forty years ago," Red told them.

"I think it's romantic," Tammy sighed. "Oh my!" Tammy stood up so fast she almost knocked the desk chair over.

Three large, strong-looking men walked into the room one at a time. The man who walked in first lifted an eyebrow as Paige shouted at Cole in the back room.

"I take it our sister is angry?"

Will stepped forward and shook his hand. "Sure is. She's something when worked up. Miles, this is my fiancé, McKenna Mason, and her friend, Danielle De Luca. This is Miles Davies, Paige's oldest brother. This is Marshall and Cade," he said as he introduced the other two men.

"So, who wants to tell us what's going on?" Miles asked.

"Don't you want to wait for them?" Dani nodded her chin in the direction of the argument.

"Nah, we'll probably get more done without those two. Who's the guy, by the way?"

"Cole Parker of the FBI."

The three brothers just nodded. It was amazing. They were all between six feet and six-two and they all had the exact same hazel eyes as Paige. They were muscular, but not bulging, steroid-type muscles. Sexy muscles they got from hard work, not pumping endless hours of iron at a gym. They varied some in the nose and jaw line, though. Miles had a square jaw, Marshall a sharp nose, and Cade had a slightly more angular face than Miles.

Kenna gave a brief rundown of what happened to her and what happened to Dani over the past four months. She showed them the note and then the picture. They were looking at the picture when Cole and Paige came back into the room.

"Miles!" She ran over and jumped into her brother's arms. Dani looked at Cole and would've sworn she heard him growl.

"Just who the hell are you and what are you doing at my crime scene?"

Ignoring Cole and looking at Paige, Miles said, "He doesn't know who we are or why we're here? Paige, you should've obtained permission."

"Sorry, Miles. When I saw that picture and when Cole said the New York Office was trying to have Kenna and Dani arrested, I just flipped out a little."

Cole gave what sounded like a snort before asking them again who they were.

"Miles Davies. Paige's older brother."

"Brother?" Cole realized he sounded pretty relieved when he immediately continued in a sterner voice. "And the rest of them?"

"This is Marshall and Cade." Miles paused for dramatic effect and then to poke fun at Cole said, "Also her brothers."

"And what does she expect her brothers to do about this?" From the smile on their faces, Dani guessed they could do a lot. There was something mysterious about her brothers.

"We have experience in these types of things. We were special forces."

Dani really tried not to laugh at poor Cole. His face was turning red and it was clear he was getting close to the end of whatever rope he was hanging onto.

"What special forces group and what kind of experience?" Cole inquired.

Poor guy. He was going to break a tooth if he kept grinding his teeth together.

"Knock it off, Miles." Marshall turned to Cole. "We started off with the Rangers. We're trained in counterterrorism. We served in Iraq, Afghanistan, and Pakistan. If there's someone you need found, we can find them."

"Started out? Where'd you end up?"

"Sorry, that's classified."

"I just bet it is. Look. I have my hands full right now trying to walk a very tight rope between legal and illegal. I'm trying to figure out a way to stall the New York office from calling in the cavalry and arresting these two."

"We can help with that."

"Sorry, which one are you?"

"Cade. I teach biology at the high school and coach football with Will."

"Oh, a science teacher is going to help me with the FBI? I don't believe this. Your whole family is nuts!"

"Give me two hours, then check the FBI database and see if there's still a bulletin out for Kenna and Danielle." Cade turned around and walked out of the office.

"Is he serious?"

"Look, we're not here to step on any toes. We're here to help. Paige has our numbers. Call us if you need us," Miles told Cole before turning and leaving with Marshall.

Dani felt Mo's hand on hers. She turned and felt horrible when she saw the stress lines around his eyes and mouth. He was so worried and it was all her fault.

"I would feel so much better if you came home with me tonight. Then I would know you were safe," Mo said with a concerned look.

"Thank you. That's very kind, but I really just want a glass of Miss Lily's special ice tea and maybe a big brownie before I go to bed. I'll be fine."

"Then at least let me walk you home. I am sure you are exhausted."

That was for sure. It was well past dinnertime now, but all she wanted was some comfort food and a good drink. She knew Miss Lily would fuss over her, but in the end give her the mothering she needed so badly right now.

"Come on then, let's get you home." He escorted her out of the room as everyone said their goodbyes.

Walking down the street, she felt the waistband of her skirt for her knife and was comforted by its feel.

"I was so scared when Will called me to tell me something had happened to you." He paused as if gathering his thoughts.

Her stomach started to flutter at the thought of being lucky enough to have someone like him care about her. It was too soon to hope he had feelings for her as strongly as she had for him. She was still amazed that love had hit her so fast.

"I was afraid I had lost you just as soon I had found you." They turned up the street and she saw the light on the porch at Miss Lily's. "I have never felt for anyone the way I feel for you. I had always thought myself cold and unfeeling, but you have changed all of that. I can't control my feelings for you. I burn for you."

Her heart lifted as she walked up the stairs. "It's the same way for me." She couldn't look at him. For some reason she was so embarrassed about her feelings. She felt Mo's hand squeeze hers as he pulled her up the last step and into his arms.

"Danielle." It was said as a plea right before capturing her lips in a passionate kiss. He pulled her closer and his hand traced the side of her body up to her face as he wiped away a tear she didn't know had fallen. "Do not fear, we can face anything if we are together." He nuzzled his head into her neck while kissing a path up to her ear.

The screen door slammed shut. She and Mo jumped apart and looked toward the noise. Miss Lily was standing in the front door with her broom in hand.

"Don't mind me, just straightening up for the night." She started humming "Camptown Races" while she swept the porch.

"How does she do that every time?" Mo whispered. Dani giggled and felt the tension from the day start to crack and fall away.

"Miss Lily, I had a rough day. I'd do just about anything for a cup of your special ice tea and a brownie." Dani smiled even more when she saw all five feet of Miss Lily puff up with pride at the compliment.

"Of course! Just let me take care of you! Come on inside and get settled."

Dani sent Mo a wink as Miss Lily herded her inside with her broom.

"Good night, Mohtadi," Miss Lily sang as she closed the front door.

# Chapter Ten

*In New York City…*

"What do you mean Chad is gone?" Pottinger yelled. He slammed the door to his large corner office and paced in front of the bank of windows overlooking the New York City skyline. Not once did he look at the pathetic excuse of an agent standing rigid before his desk. "You were supposed to keep an eye on him, Edwards."

"I am sorry, sir. I will find him." Edwards kept his eyes fixed on the framed photo of the Pottinger family that sat in the center of Gene's desk. What a hypocrite. Banging teenagers at night and then going home to his country club wife and perfect kids.

"I want him found, now. Bob thinks he went after the attorney in Kentucky. Get down there now and find him before he does something stupid, like getting caught." Pottinger rubbed his hand over his chest. This was too much stress. The heartburn was killing him. All because Bob had insisted on inviting that idiot Chad. The man was a menace, always thinking he was better and smarter than everyone. Now he was in charge of cleaning this mess up. "And Edwards, if you find Chad, kill him."

"Yes, sir." Edwards turned and left the office, quietly shutting the door behind him.

He smiled as he retrieved his car and punched Keeneston, Kentucky, into his GPS. Twelve hours from now, Pottinger would owe him big time. He could kill two birds with one stone, maybe even three birds. Take out that attorney bitch, Chad, and maybe even the assistant if she was around. That had promotion to Special Agent in Charge written all over it.

*In Keeneston…*

Since the afternoon Kenna had dropped the marriage bomb on her, Dani had been planning a surprise bachelorette party. She and Paige wanted something less formal than the engagement/wedding party Betsy was throwing, and agreed on a "Say No to the Dress: Keeneston Edition" theme.

"Shhh!" Dani held her finger up to her lips. Paige slapped her hand over her mouth to suppress the next bout of laughter from bubbling out. Dani knew Kenna endured a long day in court and was taking a nap on the couch in her office before finishing up some work. But, with her wedding just two days away, it was time for a party.

She kicked off the heels she just bought from Walmart to avoid making any noise as she crept down the hall. Dani took a deep breath to stop the contagious giggles. She and Paige tiptoed down the hall toward Kenna's office. Dani carried a bag filled with a cheap veil, a tacky wedding dress, and a lot of liquor. Paige was carrying a bag filled with food Miss Violet had prepared and a pitcher of the Rose Sisters' ice tea.

"I'm sorry, you just look so funny with that HUGE magenta bow on your ass." Paige bit down on her lip to stop from breaking into laughter again.

"Well, let's not mention the hoop skirt and layer upon layers of ruffles on your dress." Dani stopped and made the mistake of looking back at Paige. She pinched her lips together to fight the smile and silently laughed. Her shoulders shook as she took in the pale blue hoop dress with an elastic off-the-shoulder scoop top covered in white ruffles. A small parasol was hanging by a strap off her wrist. It made her magenta, fake-satin dress full of bows look good.

Dani put her hand on the doorknob and slowly turned it. She held her breath as she pushed open the door and saw that Kenna was still asleep on the couch. They crept into the room and stood before Kenna in their hideous get-ups. A laugh mixed with a little snort escaped from Paige. Dani saw Kenna's eyes shoot open as she screamed and fell off the couch. Paige and Dani succumbed to fits of laughter as Kenna stared at them in all their horrible glory.

"What's going…" Henry slid to a stop at the door and took in Kenna on the floor and Paige and Dani bent over laughing. "Those dresses are ugly as sin. But I'd still do you." He turned around and went back to his office. This time all three of them broke out into laughter.

"What are you two doing?" Kenna asked as she pulled herself up.

"Bachelorette party! We even have a dress for you." Dani pulled out the tacky dress they had bought at the thrift store.

"Do you know how drunk I'd have to be to put that on?" Kenna stared at the puffball of crinoline, netting, ruffles, and bows. It was the epitome of tacky in every sense.

"I can help with that!" Paige pulled out the pitcher of Rose Sisters' ice tea and placed it on her desk.

"No way. I won't do it."

"Come on. We'll do it with you. It's late, no one is going to find out." Dani urged Kenna toward the front door of the office. They had finished off the ice tea hours ago and had now moved on to martinis. After three drinks, Kenna had put on the hideous gown and now resembled the Michelin Tire Man. After the last round of drinks, Paige told them about the high school seniors' tradition of running naked downtown. None of them wanted to do that. So they came up with the idea to run to the courthouse and back in full wedding gear.

Dani fumbled with the lock and opened the front door. Paige took one arm and Dani took the other as they dragged Kenna out onto the sidewalk. It was well past two in the morning and Dani doubted Kenna could walk a straight line, much less run in one. However, they were having a great time. Dani's side ached from laughing so hard. Those muscles hadn't been used in months and were going to be sore tomorrow. They had laughed, danced, told embarrassing stories, and changed Henry's desktop from a picture of him with some hot woman to a picture of the three of them in their outfits.

"One, two, three. Go!" Paige took off with Kenna and Dani being dragged behind. The windows of the shops were dark, but the street lights let off a soft yellow glow. The smell of the flowers in the baskets on the light poles floated in the air as they ran down the street.

They made it to the courthouse when Kenna stopped to catch her breath. She leaned against the statue of Lady Justice astride a big horse and looked around. "This place looks so strange in the middle of the night."

"Girl, we're past middle of the night and sailing right through early morning."

Paige stood up. "Okay, last one back has to drink what the other two make. Ready, set, go!"

Dani knew she was the weakest link, but Paige was hampered by a hoop skirt and Kenna was weighed down in ruffles and bows. She took the early lead before being stopped short when she saw red and blue lights flashing from behind them.

"Come on! We were just one block away," Kenna groaned. "Now everyone is going to know about this and I'm going to blame you two."

The sheriff's cruiser pulled up along side of them and the door opened. A young man stepped out and stared momentarily before laughing outright. "Oh, I can't wait to tell the boys about this one." He reached into his pocket and pulled out a cell phone.

"Dinky, don't you dare. I'll tell your Mama about the time you ate her famous blackberry pie right before judging at the county fair, causing her to be disqualified." Paige placed her hands on her hips and tried to look intimidating in spite of the ridiculous outfit.

"Dinky? You're name is Dinky? You poor thing." Dani tried not to laugh at him, but failed.

Blushing, the boy stared first at Paige and then Dani. "It was a nickname I got during training because I ain't the biggest of people." Turning to Paige, "I don't know. This may be worth my Mama's wrath."

"Dinky, how about we make a deal?"

Dani recognized that voice. Kenna was going to negotiate. Poor Dinky.

"What kind of deal?"

"How about you don't take a picture and don't tell people about our attire and we'll help you get a new nickname."

"Deal."

Dani groaned and pulled out her sunglasses and put them on to block out the early morning sun. "Why do I have to go to court with you?"

"I want you hurting as much as I am."

"That's not nice."

"I know. But we also have to come up with a new nickname for our blackmailer."

Dani pushed open the door to the courtroom and stopped when she found everyone staring at her. When Kenna stepped through the door and stood next to Dani, there were some cheers and some moans. She grabbed her head again at the loud intruding noise.

"What is that all about?" Dani asked.

"They like to place bets on whether I'll show up to court with a hangover." Signaling to a lady who looked to be a drill sergeant,

Kenna said, "Martha, this is Danielle De Luca. She'll help me out today. Since you're smiling, I guess you won some money?"

"I learned from last time. You'll get to court no matter what. From what we heard from Dinky last night, a lot of people bet against you."

"What did Dinky say?"

"That he had to help you all walk home and that you were three sheets to the wind. He had to carry one of you."

Dani felt Kenna elbow her for the story on the new nickname. "Oh! That was me. But, you must tell me why they call him Dinky? He was anything but last night." She lowered her voice and confided in Martha. "He was as strong as a bear. So sexy when a man can take care of a woman, but to take care of three of them! You know, I used to model and he's a catch if I've ever seen one."

"A bear, you say? Dinky, sexy?"

"Sure was. I just love strong men, and that man was such a gentleman! Mmmm!" Dani gave a little sexy shiver and walked to the chair at the front table. She pushed her sunglasses back up and hoped that was enough to get the rumors started.

The Ashton Farm was lit with oriental lanterns and covered in white and red roses. Over two hundred people were enjoying drinks, food, and the unseasonably comfortable weather in Betsy and William's backyard.

Dani placed her arm on Mo's and leaned close. "You think it's time?"

"I do."

She smiled when he said those two little words while looking at her. This wedding business was really messing with her.

"Okay, I'll go send Judge Cooper out and get everything in place. Give me five minutes." She leaned over and gave him a quick kiss before running back up the stone path leading to the house.

She pushed open the big front door and yelled up the stairs, "Okay, we're ready to go in five!" She walked down the long hall and into the back living room. Peeking through the drawn curtains, she watched as Mo's men casually moved people off the stone path leading down to the back garden.

"Okay, I had to get away from Dinky, or should I say Bear. He's embracing his new rep as a sexy cop a little too much." Paige sat down on the couch and looked up to Dani. "Are they almost ready?"

"Yes. I see Mo directing Judge Cooper to the gazebo."

"Good, then all we need is my bride." Will entered the room looking stunning in a black tux. He was followed by two large men also in tuxes. "Ladies, this is Demarcus White and Daniel Goins. We played ball together in Washington. Guys, Danielle De Luca and Paige Davies. Ah, and there is my lovely bride."

Dani looked away from the mountain of men she was paired with to see Kenna come into the room. She looked gorgeous in a simple white silk gown. Will walked toward Kenna and ever so gently kissed her. Realizing she had just sighed out loud, Dani took another peek out the window. Why was she thinking about wearing a white dress herself and walking down the aisle to meet Mo? For whatever reason, the image wouldn't leave her mind tonight.

"Okay, I think we're ready. Mo just stood up with Judge Cooper on the gazebo and he's making the announcement." They were all quiet as they waited for Mo to finish talking. They knew the announcement had been made when the crowd went wild with gasps and cheers. The music was cued and she opened the door for Paige and Mountain Man to walk out first.

She quickly went to Kenna. "You look amazing. I'm so happy for you!" She kissed Kenna on her cheek and then took her place with the other Mountain Man.

"The wedding was beautiful. I can't believe we pulled that off!" She slid off her high-heeled sandals and wiggled her toes on the soft carpet of Mo's car.

"You were beautiful."

She felt her face blush at the compliment and watched as they pulled into Miss Lily's. She just couldn't shake the feeling that she was supposed to marry Mo. When she looked at him, she couldn't help but smile. That, along with the fact that her heart was jumping up and down saying 'it's him, it's him!' was a dead giveaway to how she truly felt.

Mo opened her door and bent down into her seat. "What are you doing?"

"Carrying a beautiful woman to her room." He slid an arm under her knees and another one around her back, easily lifting her out of the car. She wrapped her arms around his neck and laid her head on his shoulder. Her shoes dangled down his back from her fingertips as he carried her to the porch.

She closed her eyes and took a deep breath of his cologne. She was just too lucky. Mo was all hers. The visions from a night full of dancing lingered in her mind. They developed quickly into flashes of them married and relaxing out in the country with their kids running around them. Mo was someone who knew the city life but loved the country. He was also someone who was well traveled but ready to settle down. He was perfect.

He sat down on the swing and put his lips to hers. She snuggled into him and let the dream come to life.

"About tonight," he murmured into her hair.

The floodlight kicked on and Miss Lily opened the front door and started to sweep. She turned and jumped when she saw them on the swing. "Mohtadi!" she screeched. "I don't care if you are a prince, I'll smack you with this broom so fast if you don't stop playing hanky-panky on my porch and scaring the living daylights out of me!"

It felt like Dani's world came to a screeching halt. "Prince?"

"Um, well, the thing is," Mo's face had lost a lot color. "I am a sheik of Rahmi. But, I am third in line, so it hardly counts."

Dani jumped up. "Hardly counts? It hardly counts that you're royalty? That you have a deep obligation to your country? That we talked about raising kids in the country and finally settling down? You're a freaking prince? A prince to a country halfway around the world?"

"Don't forget you're the Most Eligible International Bachelor," Miss Lily put in.

"Oh my God." Dani shook her head. She looked out into the yard and focused on a big orange tabby cat making his way toward the house. Her visions of marriage, children, and a quiet life in the country all faded to visions of paparazzi, stuffy political dinners, and jet-setting. The tabby made its way up the stairs and hid in the dark next to the swing.

"I was going to tell you. I have just never had someone like me for me. I was selfish. I guess I should tell you all of it then. I have less than a year to be married or my father gets to choose my bride. I have five more months to marry the person of my choosing. I should also tell you that tonight I made my decision. I choose you."

Dani snapped her head around. "Oh, real nice. I dreamed of kids, a quiet life in the country, and a husband who could be my partner in life. What I get is some egotistical prince who tells me he's chosen me. You expect me to jump up and down because I'm on the top of some list? I'd rather be with that cat than someone who only wants to marry me because he's running out of time." She took a couple of steps forward and picked up the big tabby. The cat nuzzled into her hand and she absently started to scratch his head. "The worst part was that I fell in love with you. No, that's not right, I fell in love with a fantasy."

"Danielle."

"No, no more. Go polish your crown." She turned on her heel and went inside, leaving Miss Lily to close the door behind her.

She ran up the stairs and sat down hard on the end of her bed. Tears fell freely as she realized she might have ruined the best thing to happen to her. But what was real? Was the real Mo a country-living horse racer or the third in line to the crown of a whole country? She opened her eyes and realized she still had a death grip on the poor cat.

"Sorry, bud." She felt for a collar and didn't find one. Dani didn't want to face Miss Lily, so she opened the window and placed the cat on the windowsill. "There you go. I can tell you have all your claws. You can just climb down the tree and be on your way."

She slowly made her way back to bed. Her legs felt as if they were filled with lead. She was suddenly so tired. Maybe he'd come back for her? Maybe he'd fix this somehow. She curled up on top of her bed and fluffed her pillow. She felt the mattress dip and then start to vibrate. Turning her head, she saw the cat curled up next to her with his eye on the door, as if guarding her. She smiled and laid a hand on the purring cat and closed her eyes. In seconds, she was asleep.

# Chapter Eleven

"Dani? Are you in there?" The pounding resumed and Dani dragged the pillow over her head. "Dani, open up. It's Sunday. You've been hiding in here for over a day now."

Finally, there was quiet. She didn't realize it was already Sunday. What happened to Saturday? Oh well. All she knew was that the cat was still in bed with her and Mo hadn't called. He had given up, so she might as well, too.

"Dani, I swear to God, I'll shoot a hole in that door if you don't answer by the count of five."

"Go away, Paige." Dani didn't want to see anyone. She had her cat, who was currently growling at the door. And she had her fairy godmothers leaving baked goods outside of her door. There was no reason to get out of bed ever again. She sat up, though, when she heard the unmistakable sound of a shotgun being racked.

"One. Two. Three."

"Okay. Hold your fire! I'm coming. Come on, Brutus, move over." Dani pushed the cat off of her and slowly got out of bed. She unlocked the door but didn't bother opening it.

"About time. Jesus Christ! You're a mess. Come on, get undressed." Paige walked into the room and shut the door.

"I didn't know you felt that way about me."

"Ha ha," Paige replied sarcastically. "Go take a shower. Then I'm taking you out to my brother's place for some therapy."

"Therapy?"

"Yup. Shooting things. Always makes me feel better."


"Hi, Dani. Sorry to hear about you and Mo." Marshall loomed over her while trying to look sympathetic, but he still looked scary.

"Thanks. So what am I doing here?" She looked around at the field they were in. There was a huge tree with a straw dummy hanging from it. A fence had cans lined up and nothing else. They had driven past Marshall's amazing farmhouse and through a lot of cow pastures, where they had found him setting up this field.

"Since you and Mo broke up, you may be more vulnerable to attacks. I thought I could give you a refresher on that gun of yours and show you some self-defense."

"I do need the target practice. I have had plenty of self-defense in New York, though."

Marshall just smiled at the thought of Dani taking aerobics classes with a fancy name, implying they were any kind of self-defense course.

"Okay. Teach away," Dani said.

"What weapons do you normally carry?"

"I always carry my knife. I try to carry my gun, but most of the time it gets locked in the nightstand since I can't carry it into court."

"And the knife?"

"Dinky doesn't mind me carrying it. Or, he wouldn't if he ever bothered to check me." She should feel bad for sneaking a weapon into the courthouse, but she needed to feel safer.

"Okay. First, let's work on your knife usage. Then we'll go with hand-to-hand combat. When you're nice and tired, we'll try some shooting."

Marshall showed her the best places on her body to hide her knife, how to open it and use it all in one motion, and what to do after using it.

"You break him down bit by bit. Stab, kick, punch. You don't hesitate to take out a knee. You do whatever you need to do to make sure he can't get up and chase you."

He taught her correct stabbing, slicing, kicking, punching, eye-gouging, and ball-smashing techniques for hours. By the end of the practice, she felt more comfortable than ever with her knife and herself.

"Okay, shooting time." Marshall turned her in the direction of the cans and backed her up about fifteen feet.

"There's no way I can shoot. My arms are so tired they are shaking." She held up her hand to him and watched it shaking with exhaustion.

"This is the best time to practice. If you ever get into a situation where you've been in a fight, your arms *will* be shaking. As a novice, when you draw your gun, your body will be shaking with adrenalin and fear. I'll teach you to shoot that way now, so that you'll be able to hit your target if the time comes."

She nodded and took aim with her Glock. She hit two out of three, but just barely. She shot over and over again. Marshall kept handing her magazine clip after magazine clip. He had her shoot from a standing position, from the ground, and on a quick turn.

"Okay, last drill. You've done really well."

Dani felt as if the gun had been surgically attached to her shaking hand, but she had gotten better.

"I want you to close your eyes. I'm wrapping this around your eyes so you can't see. I'm going to walk you around some and then step away. I then just want you to listen and react. Got it?"

"Are you sure I won't shoot you?"

"Yes. I'll be well out of the way and you'll hear where I am." She closed her eyes and let him spin her a couple of times. He then walked her about twenty feet in one direction. "Okay. I'm walking away now. Just imagine yourself being attacked in the dark. Do what comes natural. Give me twenty seconds before you start."

She heard him walk a good distance away and stop. After he stopped, she started listening to the sounds of the outdoors. She heard a cow moo. Oh, please don't let me shoot a cow, she thought. She heard birds and the wind. Then she heard a creak right behind her and something moving. She turned and fired twice. She was knocked down by the force of the hit and her gun fell to the ground. She instantly grabbed her knife on her waistband and in one motion flicked it open and stabbed the man in the side.

"Good! Take off your blindfold." Marshall shouted as he jogged toward her. She pulled the blindfold off and saw the straw man on top of her. Marshall pulled him off and stood him up. "Very good! You shot him twice in the chest and got in a good stab with your knife. How do you feel?"

"Like every muscle is exhausted. But I feel a lot more comfortable. Thank you so much. I feel like Rambo."

"Confidence is important, just don't get too cocky. Let me know if you want to do this again. It's always good to go through a heavy practice every so often."

She gave Marshall a sweaty hug and turned to Paige. "Thanks for dragging me out of bed."

Paige looped her arm around hers and led her to the car. "No prob. But now I think a bath in Epson salt would be good for you."

Dani refrained from banging her head on the desk when the phone rang again. It was close to one hundred degrees outside, it was a full moon, and it was right after a holiday. Each of these caused mild craziness in people, but all three together was the perfect storm. Someone wanted to sue a fireworks company because he burned his hand when his friend shot him with a Roman candle. Somehow that was the fireworks company's fault, not the friend's. Another called wanting to sue his ex-wife over a bottle of Pappy's Three Year Bourbon that cost a whopping twelve dollars. And there were plenty of other calls, all involving sheer stupidity. However, she was most excited about the call for assistance on adoption.

Out of all the phone calls she got that day, she did notice the one person who didn't call her. She hadn't heard from Mo since Friday night. It was pretty clear he didn't believe she was worth fighting for.

"Hey, beautiful. You look great in that dress," Henry leaned against her door and gave her a wink.

"Thanks." She looked down at the sundress she had gotten from Target in Lexington.

"But you would look even better out of it," he gave her a little wink.

She smiled at him. "Oh, Henry. You're my favorite womanizer," she laughed and they both paused when they heard the bell ring over the door.

"Oh, please God, not another nutcase." Henry said as he hit his head against the door frame.

"Excuse me. Can I help you?" Tammy's tense voice traveled back to them. Both Henry and Dani straightened up. Tammy was never this formal.

"I'm looking for McKenna Mason and Danielle De Luca. The sign out front says this is their law office," a deep voice stated.

"It isn't their law office. It belongs to Henry Rooney." Tammy was clearly upset. Henry put his finger to his lip and motioned for Dani to be quiet. He picked up the file at the edge of her desk and walked out to the lobby.

Dani heard him enter the lobby and say, "Tammy, can you file this for me?" A couple seconds later she heard him introduce himself. "Henry Rooney. You looking for an appointment? I can squeeze you in."

"No. I'm looking for McKenna Mason and Danielle De Luca."

"Sorry. I can't help you. Kenna left town and I don't know where Danielle is. And who might you be? I can leave a message. I don't know when they'll be back, but Tammy can tell them you stopped by if they do come back."

"FBI. Special Agent Mark Edwards."

Dani stopped breathing. She didn't need to hear the rest of the conversation. She slowly slid under her desk and pulled her gun from her purse. They had come for her.

A few moments later, Henry was back at her door. "Dani. Are you in here? The guy left," Henry whispered into the room. She slowly peeked her head out from the desk and looked around. "He was an FBI agent. Apparently you were a wanted woman, but when I asked to see a warrant, he couldn't produce it. Looks like Cade knows his way around a computer. But he did leave with lots of threats about sending me to jail. Not a nice guy."

"Thank you, Henry. I better get out of here."

"I don't think so. He didn't seem to believe me when I told him you all weren't here. We'll lock up soon and turn off all the lights. You just stay put for at least an hour. I'll come back and look around, then escort you to your car. Then I want you to lock yourself up in your room at Miss Lily's with that loaded gun you have in your hand."

She looked down and realized she was still holding on to it. "Sounds like a good plan. Knock on the back door quietly so I know it's you."

The next hour and a half seemed to crawl by. Dani stayed hidden under her desk with a death grip on her gun. She heard every noise, creak, settling of the building, and movement of anyone outside. She nearly hit her head when she jumped at the sound of a quiet knock on the back door.

"Psst, Dani. I think the coast is clear. Come on." Henry stood at the back door waiting for her. "I called Miss Lily and she knows when to expect you and what's going on."

Dani wiggled out from under her desk and grabbed her purse. She walked down the hall and Henry took her arm to lead her through the dark parking lot to her car.

"You know, you aren't that bad of a guy, Henry."

"Does that mean I get thank-you sex?"

She quietly laughed and leaned over and gave him a quick kiss on the cheek. She got in the car and was about to drive away when Henry leaned into the window.

"That wasn't a 'no.' Now, get going. Miss Lily's expecting you."

Dani drove the short distance to Miss Lily's. She had never been so excited than when she saw the bright floodlights on the porch shining onto the walkway. She pulled up to the lot and parked on the other side of Miss Lily's huge Buick. She looked around and didn't see anything so she opened her car door and stood up. She looked around one more time and reached across to the passenger seat for her purse. As she pulled the purse strap over her shoulder, she heard a noise behind her. Before she could turn, a hand was placed over her mouth and an arm locked across her waist.

"Figured you'd turn up here sooner or later. Don't move. Don't fight me or I will kill you right here and now. Drop the purse." Even at a whisper, she recognized the voice. It was Agent Edwards. She tried to calm down, but it was so hard when his hand was over her mouth. She tried to breathe in through her nose but didn't feel like she was getting enough air. She dropped her shoulder and the purse containing her gun fell to the ground. Edwards kicked it off to the side.

She remembered Marshall telling her the faster you fight, the faster you're free. Taking as big a breath as she could, she lifted her foot and brought it down on his. His fingers bit into her cheek and she opened her mouth wide, clamping her teeth tight on whatever skin she could get.

"Bitch!" Edwards yanked his hand away as she sucked in a breath through her mouth. In the same instance, she screamed with all she had. Up and down the street, lights started turning on. She struggled against his arm that was still wrapped around her waist. She was so focused on getting free that she barely heard the strangest growl coming from behind her.

"Meeeeooow."

Edwards' arm relaxed around her waist enough for her to grab her knife from the leg strap under her skirt.

"Son of a bitch. Get off me, you fucking cat." Edwards kicked out with his leg and batted at his back with his arms. Dani dropped to the ground, turned, and stabbed him in the leg. "Ahhh!" A rush of satisfaction hit her as he reached for his leg while letting loose with a string of curses.

It was only then that she saw Brutus hanging from Edwards's back. His claws were extended as he gripped Edwards. He looked a lot like the Garfield doll suctioned to car windows during the early 90s. Dani scrambled around on her knees trying to reach the purse holding her Glock when she heard the unmistakable click of a gun being cocked. Looking up, she found that Edwards had shaken Brutus loose and had reached for his gun, now pointed directly at her head.

Everything in the world stopped. She didn't hear Brutus hissing, she didn't hear the sounds from the night, or the distant sound of cars. All she heard over and over again in her head was the sound of the hammer being pulled back on the gun. As she stared straight down the barrel, it felt as though her heart stopped beating and her blood stopped flowing.

"I see I finally got your attention. Toss the knife." Seeing Dani's compliance, he continued. "Good. Now, you're going to stand up and put your hands on top of your car. I'm going to cuff you and then we're heading back to New York. There are some people who are very eager to see you."

She couldn't drag her eyes away from the black barrel of the gun only inches from her face. All she could think of was all the mistakes she'd made in her life. She didn't need that extra serving of brownie the other day when she really wanted it. She wished she had told Kenna it wasn't her fault for this situation they were in. And most importantly, she hadn't told Mo she forgave him for not telling her he was royalty. That realization hit her like a ton of bricks, even with the gun in her face. She was sure he had tons of women throwing themselves at him for his money and status. After really thinking about it, she understood why he didn't tell her. If they really loved each other, then they'd find a way to make it work. She only hoped she'd live long enough to tell him.

*Click. Click.*

The noise reverberated through the night and Dani dragged her eyes away from the gun pointed at her head and up to Edwards's face. He was focused on something behind her. Oh, thank God the police must be here. She turned her head and saw a massive shotgun pointed right at Edwards's chest. Behind the shotgun was a poof of white hair.

"You don't want to do that. I am FBI and I'm here to arrest this lady. You'd be interfering with a federal officer."

Dani slowly reached out with her right hand and felt along the ground. She used her fingers to try to find the knife Edwards made her drop. She wasn't sure if Miss Lily knew how to use that gun and she figured she didn't have long to act.

"I don't care if you are Jesus Christ himself. You'll put that gun down or, bless your heart, I'll shoot you."

Dani couldn't believe that strong voice was coming from little Miss Lily. She looked up at Edwards and could tell he wasn't totally convinced to put down the gun.

"Lily Rae! What's going on over there?"

Dani looked about twenty yards behind Edwards and saw another older lady level a large .44 magnum at him. Edwards darted a glance around him as more people appeared with guns drawn.

"FBI. You are all interfering with an investigation and you will be arrested. Now lower your guns and go back to your homes."

"He's a prick, isn't he, Lil?" the older lady behind him shouted out.

"Sure is, Edna."

"I said, put down your weapons now or I will arrest all of you!" Edwards screamed, his voice cracking.

"Bless your heart, you must be one stupid son of a bitch if you expect us to do that before the police arrive. We haven't seen your badge or a warrant for that little girl's arrest," Edna told him.

Dani saw the knife out the corner of her eye, but she couldn't quite reach it. She tried shifting, but Edwards grabbed her arm so hard that she thought it would snap in two.

"You're not going anywhere. Even with your band of gun-toting grandmas, I still have the power to do whatever I want with you."

Pain shot up her arm and she saw stars dancing. They were pretty blue and red stars, though. Edwards loosened his grip as he pushed the gun against her head. She felt the cold steel pushing into her forehead.

"Sir. Put down the gun, please."

Dinky! Dinky had arrived. Oh shit, Dinky couldn't compete with Edwards. Her hopes plummeted.

"I am FBI. You have no authority here. Tell these people to lower their guns and go inside."

"Sorry, sir, we can't do that." It was a deeper voice with more twang to it. That must be Dinky's partner, Noodle. She hadn't met him but had heard about him. Two against one, maybe they could handle Edwards. "We need you to put that down and let Miss De Luca go. We'll take her into custody until you produce identification and a legal warrant for her arrest."

"No. I'm authorized by the Assistant Director in Charge of the New York Office to bring her back to New York. You're nothing but a bunch of hicks. I'll see all of you thrown in jail." He squeezed her arm tighter and she shrank into the pain. It felt as if his grip was slicing through her muscle and about to snap her arm like a toothpick. "Stop where you are or I'll shoot her right now." He drilled the gun barrel into Dani's forehead causing her to scream out in pain.

"I will give you three seconds to let her go and drop your gun."

Ahmed! Mo must be with him.

"Mo!" Dani screamed as Edwards yanked her closer to him. She bit her lip as the pain intensified.

"It's okay, love. Everything will be okay."

He was there. It sounded like he was standing next to Miss Lily, only a few yards away.

"Everything is not going to be okay. Put down those guns. I am taking her with me." He started to back up and Dani fought with all she had to break his hold.

"Last chance." The cold, steely voice hardly sounded like the Ahmed she knew.

"Or what? You'll shoot me in front of all these people? I'm an FBI agent. You'll spend the rest of your life in jail. Just who do you think you are?"

"I am Ahmed and I can shoot you and never be touched. Isn't that right, Sheik Ali Rahman?"

She felt Edwards pause. What was Ahmed talking about and why did Edwards care? She caught a movement directly behind Edwards and saw Cole quietly walking up behind them with his gun drawn. Adrenalin surged and hope soared.

"Edwards. It is not good to see you again. However, I do have great pleasure in telling you to put the gun down and place your hands behind your back. You are under arrest. And I do have a legal warrant from the Deputy Director of the FBI, not that corrupt Pottinger in New York."

"Parker!" Edwards said Cole's name as if it were a curse.

"Put the gun down."

"Never. The girl's coming with me."

Before she could scream, the sound of a gun going off filled the night air.

Edwards staggered back, still holding onto her arm. As he fell to the ground, he dragged Dani on top of him. She screamed as she saw the blood start to spread over his shirt. She tried to stand up, but Edwards still had a grip on her arm. Frantic, she clawed at his hand trying to pry it off.

"Dani! Are you okay? Oh, please tell me you're okay." Mo dropped to her side as Ahmed and Cole tended to Edwards.

"Is he... is he dead?" she asked Ahmed.

"No. I shot him twice in the arm. He'll probably lose it, but he'll live."

"Dani, answer me. Are you hurt? Did he hurt you?" Mo was scanning her for injuries.

"Get his hand off me, please." The panic hadn't subsided yet. Until she had his hand off of her arm, she wouldn't be able to relax. Mo reached down and pried it open. She fell back and on to her bottom on the driveway.

"Danielle! Oh you poor dear! Are you alright?" Miss Lily ran to her side, the massive shotgun hanging down by her side. Dani just wanted a moment with Mo to tell him she understood but was surrounded by neighbors as Ahmed, Cole, Dinky, and Noodle called ambulances and administered first-aid to Edwards.

"Where's Brutus? Brutus! Come here, boy!" she called. That cat had tried to save her and she just wanted to hold him. She felt him rub against her bare leg and scooped him up. "You're such a good boy. I'll feed you fresh fish for the rest of your life."

"You should've seen that cat! He jumped onto Edwards's back and dug in with all of his claws. He caused Edwards to drop his lock on Dani and she stabbed him in the leg," Miss Lily told all of the onlookers.

"Dani! Oh my God. Are you okay?" Paige pushed her way through the crowd with Marshall and Miles. Dani grabbed Mo's hand and looked him in the eye. She hoped with that look she conveyed her feelings to him since she couldn't tell him now.

"Can you please help me up?" She placed her hand in his and gave a little squeeze. She saw his eyes soften as he rubbed his thumb across her knuckles. "I'm okay, just let me stand up."

He nodded and stood up. He held out his hands and helped pull her up. Her legs felt wobbly after being pinned underneath her for so long.

"Thank you, everyone. I'm okay. I can't thank you enough for saving me."

"Oh! Bless you heart, come here before I start leaking like a watering pot." Miss Lily wrapped her arms around her and hugged her tight.

"Sweetheart, the EMTs are here. Let them check you out. I'll hold Brutus for you." Turning around, she saw Edwards being loaded into one ambulance. Cole and Noodle went with him.

Dani was being checked over in the other ambulance when Mo asked, "Can I take her home?"

"Yes, but make sure she gets some rest and plenty of food and water. She's had a major shock. Her forehead will be bruised for a couple of days. Her arm suffered deep abrasions and will most likely take weeks to heal. Try not to use it for a couple of days." The EMT took the blood pressure cuff off and started packing his first-aid kit.

# Chapter Twelve

---

Mo placed Brutus on a towel in the back seat of the Mercedes and scratched his ears. "I'll have the cook prepare you some salmon."

Brutus purred and rubbed his head against Mo's hand, happy with his upcoming treat. Mo opened the front door and slid into the seat. He cast Dani a look that she knew meant he was unsure of where he stood with her.

"Mo. There's something I need to say without being interrupted."

He nodded and stared out the windshield into the dark night as he drove toward his farm. Maybe it would be easier to say when he wasn't focused on her.

"This afternoon I spent an hour and half under the desk in my office." She saw him whip his head toward her with his eyebrow raised. "I thought about what you told me, about it being the first time someone liked you for you, and that was why you didn't tell me who you are. Well, I thought about it and I understand it. I thought about this last week together. There were no paparazzi, no women falling at your feet, and plenty of privacy. If we both care for each other, we can overcome any obstacle. That is, if you do care for me that way." Suddenly feeling vulnerable, she looked out the window as they turned into Desert Sun Farm.

A huge house came into view. No, it wasn't a house — it was a palace. It was three stories high and made of red brick. There was a

Greek revival entrance and two large wings that went off from the sides of the main part of the house. There had to be at least twenty stairs heading to the front door from the ornately red colored graveled driveway.

"I guess that's your farmhouse I kept imagining?" She spoke with a mixture of awe and trepidation. How could a place like that be a home?

"I must be completely honest with you. There has been a woman here the past two days. That is why I could not come see you. And I must admit I didn't think you wanted to see me."

"A woman!" That was fast. Here she sat trying to see if they could work things out and he had moved on in a matter of hours.

"Wait. It's not what you think. You remember me telling you that in five months I must marry or my father will choose for me?" He waited for her to nod before continuing on. "Well, every couple of weeks he sends a woman of his choosing. They stay the night until I can ship them back. Kenna calls them The Bachelorettes. I call them a pain in the ass. But, since some of their fathers are high-ranking officers in government or royalty, I can't just tell them to get lost. Please tell me you understand."

"Where do they stay when they are here?"

"Well, you see that far left wing?"

"Yes."

"That is my private wing. They stay in the back of the far right wing. I must warn you. They will keep showing up until I am married." As Mo climbed out of the car and walked around to open her door, she closed her eyes and thought about the situation. Was the love she was feeling enough to overcome a domineering father, Bachelorettes, and the other downfalls to being royal? The answer was simple and it came to her quickly.

The house was even bigger than her parents' sprawling villa in Italy. Black and white marble floors and beautiful paintings gave the house a luxurious feeling. But Mo had worked hard at making it comfortable as well. The paint colors were warm and the furniture inviting.

He stopped in front of a huge staircase that went up a story and then divided with one branch going off to the left and the other to the right, leading to a wraparound balcony on the second floor that overlooked the entrance hall. "I am not very good at this. I am afraid I am making horrible mistakes." He shifted from one foot to the other as he tried to decide on his words. "See, I have always been pursued for my status and money. No one bothered to find out who I was and what I wanted. As a result, I have never been in love or able to express any kind of feelings. Actually, I am pretty sure my father would forbid it."

Mo stopped again and took a deep breath in an obvious attempt to fight off frustration. Dani grabbed her hands to prevent herself from throwing them around him and begging him to love her.

"If we have any hope of a future, then we must always be honest with each other. I fell in love with you when Kenna told me about you."

Dani bit down on the corner of her lip to keep from saying anything. She didn't want to miss a word.

"I must tell you, as soon as I met you, I ordered an investigation on your background. But I never opened the report. You were such a gift to me that I wanted to unwrap you layer by layer myself. As I have done so, I have found that I am falling more and more in love with you."

Dani's heart swelled and all her nerves disappeared. She knew it was right. They made sense together.

"I love you, too. I didn't know it was possible to feel the way I do. When I didn't have you beside me, the world just didn't seem as bright." She smiled as she watched Mo's expression turn from nervous to excited.

He closed the distance and kissed her with such passion that Dani couldn't hold anything back. They were fighting to show how much they loved one another through this one kiss. Her toes were curled and their bodies couldn't get close enough.

She laughed when he swept her up into his arms and carried her upstairs. She didn't notice the priceless art on the walls or the crystal chandeliers. All she saw was the love he had for her in his eyes.

Dani slowly woke as the sunlight came into the room. They had forgotten to close the curtains last night. There had been other things on their minds. She grinned and thought about closing them now, but that would mean having to move Mo's arm and leg that were thrown over her. Brutus was happily curled up on his own chair by the window watching birds.

"Hmm, good morning, love." Mo kissed her neck and pulled her closer to him.

"Mo, tell me what it's like being royal." Maybe if she knew what to expect she wouldn't be so nervous about their future together.

"It's horrible. I won't lie. There are so many expectations on you, but you have to be true to yourself. I grew up in a very strict home. Love was not commonplace, decorum was. That's why I want a wife I love and why I want to raise my children here without so many pressures on them. I will never be totally free from duty, though. There are meetings and events in Rahmi that I must attend. If I am fortunate enough to marry a woman of my choice, then I hope she would choose to come with me when I must travel. What was it like for you growing up?"

"I was lucky. I had a very loving and supporting family. Hugs, kisses, and celebrations for every milestone were normal in the De Luca household. I enjoyed seeing the world, but the only thing I'd change was that I longed for one home. That's why I want one so badly now. A loving home where I could raise my family." Dani linked her fingers through Mo's and brought his arm around her. She snuggled into his warmth and basked in the feel of him. She glanced up and looked around the room for the first time. It was a light tan color with a massive bed covered in the softest white fabric she had ever felt. The room had a fireplace, balcony, sitting area, a massive flat screen, and a separate room that was the closet next to the bathroom. Looking over at the nightstand, she saw a book Mo was reading and the clock.

"Oh crap. It's already nine o'clock. We have a client coming into the office soon. I gotta go." She jumped up and started searching the room for her clothes.

"I will call Ahmed. He will stay with you today. You will be safe with him."

"What's up with Ahmed? Why does just his name elicit fear in the FBI?"

"Ahmed is a trained soldier in my country. He is known for his interrogation techniques and his cold nature. He is fearless and will do whatever needs to be done to complete the mission. He is one of the main reasons our country has remained independent and not fallen under the control of one of the larger nations."

"Wow. I'd never have guessed. Why is he with you and not back in Rahmi?" She picked up her skirt and stepped into it while scanning the room for her panties.

"His brother is in control of our country's armed forces now. Ahmed had been undercover for a couple of years and was ready for a break. After Ahmed foiled a plan to blow up our pipelines, my father rewarded him with this job. He has complete control over all security in the United States."

After she slipped on her shoes, Dani brushed her fingers through her hair before quickly putting it into a ponytail. She ran over to the bed and kissed Mo. It was hard leaving him naked in bed, but her adoption client was coming in to fill out some paperwork for the social worker.

"I'll see you later."

*In New York City…*

Gene Pottinger grabbed another antacid from the bowl sitting on his desk. There was a brief knock at his door before it opened and Federal Judge Brian Voggel stepped in.

"What is this frantic phone call about, Gene?"

"Wait until Jarred and Dick get here," he answered before reaching into the candy bowl again for another antacid.

"Here they come now," Voggel nodded to where Felting and LeMaster were approaching the door.

"What's the big deal, Pottinger? I have a murder trial in thirty minutes," Voggel said as he took a seat in a leather chair facing the bank of windows overlooking the city.

"Not me. I cleared my calendar for this 'crime prevention task meeting.' The mayor was thrilled that I'm getting involved. When this is done, I'm going to 'get involved' with that cute coffee girl downstairs," Felting chuckled.

"Shut up, Jarred. We have a major problem. The Lexington office called this morning to let me know Edwards was killed in a robbery yesterday evening." Pottinger watched the mood shift in the room.

"What was Edwards doing in Lexington? I thought he was gathering evidence against Chad?" LeMaster asked as he took a seat next to Voggel.

"Chad disappeared and I am positive he went after that attorney in Kentucky since he was having no luck finding the assistant here. I sent Edwards down there early yesterday morning to clean this mess up. The Lexington office said he stopped for gas an hour north of Lexington and was killed when he tried to stop a burglary in process. I pulled his credit card records and saw where he purchased the gas. It looks like he went inside to pay and interrupted some thug holding up the clerk. Edwards tried to draw his weapon and the thug fired. At least, that's the story the Lexington newspaper says. Sounds like something Edwards would do." Pottinger moved the picture of his family aside and thought about the hot piece of ass he was banging at the time Agent Parker had interrupted with the news. Damn Edwards for messing everything up.

"We were going to have to get rid of Edwards anyway. This is a blessing in disguise. Now we just have to take care of Chad and the women." LeMaster brushed imaginary lint off his pant leg as he stood up. "Let's just go forward with Plan B. Voggel, can you arrange it?"

"Of course. I think I have the perfect man in mind. I'll let you know when I get the details finalized. Now, I have to get going. Gentlemen." Voggel shook hands and walked out the door whistling a peppy beat under his breath.

*In Keeneston…*

"Ahmed. Stop scowling. You're scaring off our clients," Tammy chided. "Dani, every person who comes in the door is patted down and glared at. I know he's eye candy, but geez, he's scary eye candy." Tammy gave him a once-over as she complained.

"I'm just seeing to your safety." Dani could've sworn she saw a slight blush in his face when Tammy called him eye candy and had trouble not laughing.

"How about this; Marshall Davies has his own private security company. How about we see if he can take the afternoon shift?"

"I will check with Mo and let you know." Ahmed stood up and walked outside.

"Would you look at that butt?" Tammy sighed and placed her chin in the palm of her hand as she blatantly checked Ahmed out.

"Tammy!"

"What? He's so sexy in that dark and dangerous way. I could look at him all day if he'd stop scaring off the clients."

Ahmed put the phone in his pocket and walked back inside. "Marshall said he'd provide security from now on."

Dani felt horrible. It wasn't like he was doing a bad job. He was actually doing such a good job that no one wanted to get near them.

"Thank you, Ahmed. You are simply too good at your job." Dani gave him a hug and a quick kiss on the cheek.

"Don't forget about me. I want to thank you for keeping me safe, too!" Tammy jumped up and ran around the desk. Her new pale-green highlights shimmered in her blonde hair. She grabbed Ahmed and gave him a hug. One hand resting on his chest and the other one slid down and grabbed a handful of butt. "Hmm. I am going to miss you." Tammy let go and walked back to her desk with a huge smile.

Dani looked at Ahmed and couldn't believe the size of a smile he had on his face. Apparently, Henry had an apprentice.

Dani was researching adoption procedures and writing a memo for Kenna when Tammy flung herself dramatically through the door. "I can't take it. They just keep getting hotter and hotter."

"What are you talking about?"

"Our new bodyguard," she fanned herself and pretended to swoon.

"I never thought I'd say this, but girl, you need to get laid."

"You're preaching to the choir." Tammy got up and pranced out of the office and back to her desk.

When Dani got done with the research, she wanted to go thank Marshall for the lessons. She was sure they helped her greatly. The bell rang over the door and then rang again and again. After a couple of minutes it rang again. Not being able to focus with the rising hum of noise coming from the lobby, she decided to take a break and go talk to Marshall. She walked around the corner and stopped. The lobby was filled with women. Some in jeans, some in outfits fit for a garden party. One consistency, though, was the flirty looks they kept sending Marshall. Henry was in the conference room looking like he had died and gone to heaven while working his way through the line of women.

Dani walked up to Tammy and whispered to her. "What is going on?"

"Well, in Keeneston the Davies brothers are something of legend. They raised hell and broke hearts when they were younger. Then they went off to the military and came back as decorated heroes. They are the most eligible men in town. Word got out that Marshall was hanging out here and the women came flocking to try to get his attention. I swear this has been the most fun I've ever had at work."

Dani slowly worked her way through the crowd of women vying for Marshall's attention and sat down beside him. She sat next to him on the loveseat and rubbed the top of her foot. She counted at least four women who had stomped their pretty heels onto her foot as she tried to make her way to Marshall's side.

"Thank you for your lessons. I don't think I'd have been able to keep my head without them."

Marshall leaned over and gave her a hug. The mood in the room shifted, and suddenly she was in fear for her life again. The group of women gave her the eye and began plotting among themselves.

"Are you ready to head home?" Marshall asked. A chorus of outraged noise filled the lobby.

"You better get me out of this safely," Dani whispered to him.

"Fine. You're no fun," he whispered back. He cleared his throat to gain the attention of every woman there. "I best get you back to your boyfriend." The mood instantly shifted, bringing back smiles and adoring eyes. Dani shook her head and walked back to get her things. She knew she was leaving early, but it had just been too weird of a day.

Marshall watched her climb the stairs of Mo's house before driving off. She opened the door and walked into the foyer. She closed her eyes and enjoyed the lack of humidity for a second. When she opened her eyes, an older man was walking toward her. He was dressed in an expensive suit and his face was cold. She looked down at her tan sandals from Payless and her pink sheath dress from the Dress Barn and instantly felt inadequate.

"What do you want? What are you doing here?" he demanded. Dani recoiled and backed up against the wall.

"I'm here to see Mo. Who are you?"

"There is no Mo here. There is only His Highness, Mohtadi Ali Rahman. You are certainly not here to see him. You are here to con your way into his bed, his bank account, and his title."

Ah, Mo's father. She wondered if Mo even knew he was here. Dani regretted not calling first, but she was too excited to see him again. And now, she was face to face with a bitter old man. If anything, she felt sadness upon meeting him. She was sad that Mo had to grow up under such a domineering and unhappy parent.

"You are nothing… nothing to my son and certainly nothing to me. You do not know how to be a proper wife or even a proper lady. You would be an embarrassment. You are just selling yourself in hopes of landing it rich," he continued his attempt to degrade her.

She almost smiled at that. She was a very rich woman. If he had done any research into her instead of just assuming, he would've easily found out she was the sole heir to the De Luca Winery. It may be a small winery compared to the factories that put out hundreds of millions of bottles of cheap wine, but it was still lucrative. Her father's wines started out at five hundred dollars a bottle and went up into the thousands. She hadn't looked at her trust fund since she turned eighteen and vowed not to touch it until she was thirty. However, nine years ago it had over $30 million in it.

"You drive a car that is nothing but trash, just like you. You are here only a day and already you have a chauffeur driving you around at my son's expense. You are a parasite."

It was one thing to criticize her, but to criticize her car was something completely different. She had worked hard for that car and it was a symbol to her parents and to the world that she wasn't a spoiled rich girl who was lucky enough to be born into one of the oldest family wineries in the world. That car was a testament to her character.

"Enough. You've already made incorrect assumptions about me, and that's fine. That just shows your lack of intelligence and good manners. But I will no longer listen to you degrade me and everything I've worked hard for."

The man was clearly not used to a woman talking back, and especially insulting him. His face grew bright red.

"Father! Just what do you think you are doing?" Mo stormed into the entranceway, fury radiating off of him.

"I am ridding your house of this garbage."

"Father, you are leaving right this instant." Mo spoke slowly but clearly as his hands clenched into fists.

"Mo. No, I can go to Miss Lily's. I won't come between you and your father."

"No, Danielle. He will not speak to any guest in my house like that. Father, please leave. We will conclude our talks tomorrow morning when I have calmed down." Not waiting for his father to leave, Mo held out his hand for Danielle to take. When she did so, he pulled her along the hallway, never once looking back at his father.

# Chapter Thirteen

o didn't stop walking until he was in his study with the door closed and locked behind him. He paced back and forth in an obvious effort to control his anger. "I am so sorry. My father is an uncaring man."

"Mo, it's okay. I understand. If you think about it, he really was just looking out for your best interests. He just doesn't think I'm in your best interest."

"I only wish he cared that much. No, he's here because he wants me to marry the daughter of a Saudi oilman. He hopes to combine our wealth through a deal with him. In exchange for the girl becoming a princess, my father will receive an oil production company on the mainland. He's not worried about my best interests. He's worried about his business deal." Mo ran his hand through his dark hair and sat down beside her on the couch.

Some strands fell forward across his forehead and Dani pushed them back with her fingers. Her stomach plummeted at the thought of Mo being sold off for a business deal. The thought of Mo being married off to someone else squeezed her heart in the most painful of ways.

"Come here, Mo." She leaned back on the couch and opened her arms. Mo fell into her, kissing her with all the anger, frustration, and hurt his father had caused him. She kissed him back with all the love she had. His hand ran up her calves and slipped under her knees. He lifted up her legs and laid them on the couch, never breaking his kiss.

"I need you so badly right now."

"It's a good thing I'm here then," Dani said as she kicked off her shoes and slipped out of her skirt.

"Don't go to work today. Spend the day with me." Mo tugged down the sheet and kissed a trail from her ear to her breasts. After spending hours in the study, they had finally made their way to Mo's bedroom late last night. She certainly had a new appreciation for the furniture Mo selected after last night.

"You have that meeting with your father."

"I am to meet with him shortly. Stay in bed. Relax. I will send up breakfast. Before you are done, I will have completed my business with my father. Then we'll spend the whole day together doing whatever you wish."

"Okay. You've talked me into it. Mo," She bit down on the side of her lip. "Your father wasn't completely wrong about me, you know. I may have many layers for you to unravel, but one thing I am not is royalty. I am not used to international gatherings, I am not political, I'm not trained in deportment or how to throw a dinner party," she stopped. Although it hurt, she had to admit her inadequacies. "Through my own stubbornness, I turned down financial help from my parents when I was eighteen. They had offered me money, but I had to provide them details on how I spent it and obtain their permission to use it until I was twenty-five. I told them I didn't need the money and that I wouldn't touch it until I was thirty. They were upset. But I think my mom, especially, was proud of me. So I took odd jobs and modeling gigs to pay for college. I was working to live on my own while the women your father is putting before you were trained every day of their lives for the job of being your wife. There's no way I can compare to them." Dani pulled the bed sheet up as she felt she had revealed an undiscovered part of herself to him.

She watched as he paused in the act of getting dressed and looked at her. He was upset. She hung her head, knowing the break-up was coming. He had realized she was not the same caliber of woman his father's choices were.

He walked over to her and stopped in front of her. "Dani, look at me."

She looked at his socks and slowly made her way up his slate-gray trousers to his bare chest. Oh, she was going to miss him. She didn't know how she'd make it through a day without him. She brought her eyes up to his face and saw that his mouth was strained.

"Danielle, if I cared one bit about deportment and how to throw a dinner party, don't you think I would have married already? I know that my father upset you, and that was exactly what he was trying to do. He was trying to make you feel inadequate so that you'd leave and he could save his business deal." Mo bent down in front of her and took her hands in his. He gently clasped them, running his thumb over her hand. He looked her in the eye and brushed the hair back from her face. "I love you. Nothing is going to change that."

"Oh Mo!" She flung her arms around his neck and buried her head in his shoulder. "I love you, too. I know I'm not what your parents wanted, but I'll try to do everything right. Just tell me what I need to do."

"All you need to do is be yourself. I need to get to this meeting now." Kissing her on her forehead, he rose and slipped into a white button-up shirt. "Think about what you'd like to do today. I'll be back before you know it."

Dani got out of the largest tub she'd ever seen and toweled off. She was about to go in search of clothes to borrow when she saw the extra bag from her car on the bed. Someone must have brought it up while she was soaking in the tub from heaven. She pulled out a white tank top and a pair of jeans after rifling through the bag.

She tried to remain occupied while she waited for Mo to return, but as every minute passed she got more and more nervous. What if his father had been able to change Mo's mind? She was just about to call her mother to ask for advice when Mo walked into the room.

He smiled and headed over to her. He didn't appear upset, so maybe the meeting went well. "How did it go?" She couldn't wait any longer, she had to know. Mo had told her not to worry about his father's opinion, but a part of her did care.

"Exactly what you probably expected. Posturing, yelling, lecturing, guilt…all of the normal stuff for a royal family meeting. He was not too pleased about the business deal falling through but has developed a plan to put it on hold until I am officially out of the running. He won't believe it until he sees me married. As you know, dating is not enough. He doesn't understand that what we have is more than a casual date or two, but rather a lifetime just beginning."

"Mo, are you proposing?" Dani was pretty sure he could hear her heart about to jump out of her chest.

"No," he smiled at her. "You will know my proposal when you see it."

Now she knew her heart was definitely about to jump out of her chest. He had said when, not if. She almost jumped up and down at the thought of being Mo's wife. To wake up every morning with him, to have him as her partner, and to raise their children together would be a dream come true.

"So, have you thought about what you wanted to do today?"

"Actually, I have two ideas. Do you own a pair of jeans?"


Dani grabbed Mo's hand and raced through the front door. She laughed when he came out of his dressing room in a white button-up shirt and jeans with sharp creases down the front. At least he had tennis shoes. By the end of the day, she planned to have him wrinkled and smiling.

"I want to see your little farm here."

"We'll never be able to walk it all. You want to ride in the truck or take some horses?"

"Horses! I haven't ridden in such a long time." Dani couldn't stop the huge grin and felt like clapping and jumping to show her excitement.

"Come on. There are a couple of retired geldings in the closest barn," Mo pointed to a barn about a quarter mile from the house.

The house was elevated on one of the numerous gently rolling hills seen throughout Central Kentucky. Mo had landscaped the backyard with a beautiful walking garden filled with roses, a fish pond, wildflowers, statues, and a fountain. She could spend hours exploring all the nooks and crannies in the garden that took up a couple acres.

"Past this first barn, which I call the retirement home, is the mare barn to the left and the foaling barn to the right. There are plenty of pastures separating all the barns. Then we have the stud barn, and back near the manager's house is the sick barn. The practice track and the barns housing the horses in training are further back."

Dani looked around the landscape of the farm. Manicured pastures dotted with horses and outlined with black fences stretched as far as she could see. In the far distance, the green of the grass seemed to melt into the blue of the sky. It was simply breathtaking.

They approached the barn Mo referred to as the retirement home. The barns were beautiful and new. They were *I*-shaped, housing the horses in the middle. The left wing held the offices and the right wing contained break and tack rooms. All the barns were a dark ivory with angular green roofs and large green doors. Flowers were planted in old bourbon barrels on each side of the stable doors. Large, leafy trees surrounded the barns, helping to keep them cool in the summer heat.

"There's Snow Bunny and Spot," Mo pointed out as they stopped next to two stalls. "If you couldn't guess, one of my nieces named these two."

Dani peeked into the first stall to see an all-white horse with one black dot right above her tail. It did kinda look like a bunny tail. The other horse was a no-brainer. He was a beautiful boy with white and chestnut spots all over. "They're great. I'll take Bunny. She looks really sweet." She reached her hand through bars on the stall door and let Bunny check her out.

Mo opened the stall door and led Bunny to the tack room. While she held onto Bunny's bridle, Mo saddled her and went to get Spot. Soon they were on their way around the property. It had been a long time since Dani had been on a horse, but it was hard to forget. Her body relaxed as they moved up to a gallop. She felt the second it all came back to her. Her body started to move as one with the horse. She glanced over at Mo and almost fell off Bunny. There was something about a man on a horse. His black hair was loose around his ears, flowing back as he picked up speed. He turned and smiled at her and Dani realized that she had never been happier.

She and Mo galloped over the unimposing hills and took a quick turn around the practice track before heading back to the barn. The farm was large and completely devoted to raising horses, unlike Will's farm that had some corn, cows, and hay. After Bunny was unsaddled and washed down, Dani loaded a small cooler into one of the farm trucks and herded Mo into the cab.

"Where are we going now?" Mo asked.

"It's a surprise. It's something I grew up doing and loved. I thought I'd share it with you."

"Do I get a hint?"

"Nope." Dani grinned as she headed toward the Mountain Parkway.

"Come on, this isn't so bad, is it? Look how beautiful it is." Dani gestured to the wide expanse around them.

"I must admit, it is amazing. This is the first time I have ever hiked. But, this," he gestured to their surroundings, "is something I have never seen. Where did you find it?"

"I called Paige and asked her for a nice place to hike. She recommended Natural Bridge."

Dani and Mo stood in the middle of a naturally formed sandstone archway connecting the top of two mountains. They had walked through the forest and up the original trail to the bridge. The wind was strong on top of the mountains and the views were amazing. From atop the bridge, she saw the ridges of the Appalachian Mountains stretching out as far as the eye could see.

"So what do you think of hiking?"

"I think it could be addicting. There is no pressure out here, only freedom. Thank you for introducing me to it."

She watched as Mo looked around at the large rock formations and out over the tops of thousands of acres of trees. "Ready for the three-mile hike back down?"

"Not quite yet."

He wrapped an arm around her waist and wrapped his fingers around the back of her neck, guiding her face toward his. It was dangerous to take this any further while on top of a windy stone bridge with no rails, so she didn't leap on him like she wanted. But the second they got home would be another story. She felt his hand run down her arm as he laced his fingers with hers.

"Now I am ready." He winked at her, flooding her mind with thoughts of what could be. "Are you okay? Your face is rather flushed."

"Um. No. I'm fine. Come on, let's take this path down." They walked hand in hand over Natural Bridge and started down the dirt path. "What is being royal really like for you? I mean, I know you don't like it that much, but there must be something good to come of it. Right?"

"Well, it's both the best thing and worst thing that ever happened to me. It has provided me with money to do anything I have ever wanted, like my racing stable. But it has also prevented me from enjoying the real world. I can attend gallery openings, vacation at the most exclusive resorts, and so on. But it doesn't allow me to meet people and have friends. As I told you before, I never had a friend other than Ahmed. I would have never gone hiking! I always have to put on a smile, talk to reporters, and see my private life splashed on the front page of the international papers. The best thing I ever did was move to Kentucky. Here, they don't care if you're wealthy or who you date."

"Ha! That's what you think. I was told one of the reasons people were wary of you in the beginning was because of the many different women who showed up at your house each week. It seems they didn't care that you were rich. They cared you were a man-slut." Dani started laughing at Mo's shocked expression.

"How did they know about the women?"

"One thing both Kenna and I have learned is this town has an information network that would make Ahmed jealous!"

"Well, hopefully there will only be one woman coming to my house from now on."

Hope soared in Dani's heart at the same time her stomach got a little nervous. She was torn between the excitement of falling in love and the feeling that they were moving too fast. She didn't know whether to jump for joy or hide under a rock.

"Will you tell me more about this deal you have with your father? I don't want to come between you and your family." When Mo showed signs of protest, she continued, "I know you aren't close, but I would like to change that. I have a very close family and love that my parents will always be there for me if I need anything. Maybe even be there a little too much, but I have their love and support. You should have that, too. But, if they can't stand me, then it'll just cause stress in our relationship."

"I am my parents' youngest child. I am also the last one unmarried. My sisters were married off first. Then my oldest brother, who is heir to the throne of Rahmi, was married off next so he could get started on a family. Then the middle brother married. That left just me. My father had so many offers for the last Ali Rahman that he didn't know which one to take. He tried to get me to marry a woman from France whose father is very wealthy. He sells petroleum. I refused because I was only turning thirty and not ready to settle down. I've been told what to do all of my life and I wanted freedom. So I refused to agree to the marriage and told my father I wanted some time away from Rahmi. An epic battle took place and finally my mother sat us both down to negotiate. She agreed I should be able to marry whomever I want. She had been forced into marriage with my father and didn't want the same for me. She helped persuade my father to give me some time and set the limit at five years.

"At thirty, five years seemed like forever. I thought I could easily meet someone and fall in love. What I did not count on was the press picking up the story and ranking me in all these bachelor polls with a blurb on how I must marry within five years or be disowned. That part is untrue. I will not be disowned. I will have to marry one of the women my father selects. We set out the terms and both signed the legal documents. For the past four years, I have been avoiding the women I meet since they all seem to be after one thing and one thing only — money. They do not care for me. They only care for the title they will get when they marry me." Mo paused on the trail and looked around at the trees and rocks surrounding him.

"The deal stated as long as I made a formal engagement, according to the laws of Rahmi, before my thirty-fifth birthday, my father had to honor the marriage. My birthday is exactly five months from now, December 7th."

"What does a formal engagement entail?"

"My parents would need to meet you. You would have to undergo a physical examination by a doctor to determine you are in good health. You will be tested for genetic diseases that would hinder your ability to have children or that could be passed down to any children, diminishing their ability to rule the country. You will also undergo a psychiatric evaluation to determine if you are mentally stable. After the doctors have conducted these tests, which should only take a short amount of time, my father and mother will issue a royal proclamation that will be sent to the media for publication."

She had stopped on the hill and unable to move. That was a lot more than saying "yes" at the right time. She knew she didn't have anything to worry about with the tests, but it felt degrading knowing you had to go through them. She felt more like a potential horse for sale than a wife.

"Dani, I know it's a lot to ask, but I will be with you every step of the way."

"Are you sure you're not proposing? Because I think you need to remember I haven't said yes yet." She spun on her heel and started down the trail again. Soon enough she heard him running after her.

"I am sure, this isn't a proposal. I told you before—you will know it when you see it. What I want to know is, are you prepared for this? Do you think you can handle these tests and more importantly, do you love me enough to do them?"

She continued walking down the trail but threw out her arm and smacked him in the stomach. "Of course I love you enough to do them. If by doing them, I help smooth the relationship between you and your father, then I'll do them twice. I'll do them even though it'll feel like a horse on the auction block."

"That's just one of the reasons I love you."

Mo opened the car door for Dani and helped her out. He slipped his hand into hers as they started up the stairs to Mo's home. Dani leaned close to him as all the sexy thoughts she had for the past two hours were about to come true.

"You know what I've been thinking about?"

"No. What?"

"You and me naked in that huge bathtub."

"You know what I have been thinking?"

"Hmmm?"

"I have been thinking of doing this to you." Mo spun her toward him and kissed her hard and fast. His tongue pushed past her lips and caressed her mouth. Dani grabbed hold of his waist as he pushed the front door open. His mouth never left hers. He wrapped his arms around her and guided her through the door. His hands slid lower until he could grab her bottom and pull her tight against his erection.

"Danielle Isabella Darina De Luca! What are you doing with that man's hands all over you?"

Dani and Mo jumped apart. Mo shoved her behind him to protect her from the unknown threat. Dani stood on her toes and looked over Mo's shoulder to the tall, olive skinned man with gray hair standing before them.

"Papa?"

She could feel the moan coming from Mo as he released his hold on her. She was about to run to her father when she heard another voice.

"Bella?" A beautiful blonde woman with bright blue eyes came out of the sitting room and stood next to Dani's father. "Oh my." Her face flushed as she caught sight of Mo's tented pants. "Come on, Anthony, let's give them a moment." She reached for her husband's arm, but he jerked it away.

"I want to know who this *stronzo* is with his hands all over my daughter."

If this didn't kill the mood any faster, Dani didn't know what did. She stepped out from behind Mo and placed her hand on his arm.

"Papa, Mama, this is Mohtadi Ali Rahman, my boyfriend. Mo, this is my mother, Mary De Luca, and my father, Anthony De Luca."

"It is such a pleasure to meet you both. Dani has told me so much about you two." He held out his hand and shook her mother's hand. When he reached toward her father's hand, he paused. Mo's brows came together as he stared at her father. "Wait. Are you Tony De Luca, owner of De Luca Winery?"

"Kissing my ass is doing nothing to warm me to the fact you had your tongue down my daughter's throat."

"Papa!"

"Sir, I assure you I am not trying to soften you up; it's just that I have worked with a Tony De Luca, owner of De Luca Winery, before. I have conducted business with him over the phone but never met him in person. I thought you were him; excuse my mistake."

"You have?" Both Dani and her mother asked at the same time.

"Yes. De Luca Winery always donates a bottle of wine to be auctioned off for my charity, World of Difference. I am sorry for the confusion. I just thought it might be the same person."

"It is I. I know who you are, sheik. It still does nothing to negate the fact you were pawing my Bella!"

"Wait! Papa, you know Mo?"

"Of course I know him. He's an international playboy. The better question is what is he doing here with you?"

Dani watched her mother come over and grab her father's arm. She leaned over and whispered in his ear. Her mother was always the calm one. Dani and her father were the ones with tempers.

"Mo, if I may call you that, how about we go sit in that lovely sitting room and get to know each other." Her mother let go of her father and placed her hand on Mo's arm, gently guiding him into the room filled with beautiful Impressionist artwork on the white walls. They moved past the Renoir and stepped onto the thick Oriental rug.

Dani's parents took a seat in the two silk-covered armchairs before her mother started talking again. "You mentioned a charity; what does it do exactly?"

"We raise money to help provide transportation and living expenses for families who have a child in need of specialized medical care. Care that cannot be provided in that country. We set up volunteer doctors and hospitals and then work with the government to arrange for the child and family to fly to the hospital and obtain whatever treatment they need."

"That sounds wonderful. I will also start donating. I can donate private skiing lessons and a week's stay at my husband's resort in Maine. Now, Tony, have you calmed yourself enough to listen to your daughter?" When she received a grunt in response, Mary stood up and turned to her daughter and enveloped her into a fierce hug. "I have missed you so much. I know we said we'd wait until the end of the month, but I just couldn't do it. I am ready to hear everything." Her mother released her from the hug and looked her right in the eyes. "Do you understand, Bella? Everything."

Dani nodded her head and sat down next to Mo on the loveseat facing her parents. Well, she'll tell them everything… to an extent. She started with the night of Kenna's birthday and then moved on to the months she spent in New York tracking the people who were hunting her. She ended with the incident at Miss Lily's and the fact that Ahmed and Cole were interviewing Agent Edwards today.

"I hope they tear him limb-from-limb," Mary said as she sat back in her chair and crossed her legs.

"Mama! I have never heard you wish ill on someone before."

"That's before they messed with my baby. You don't think I taught you all those things in the wilderness just for you to take your pictures, do you? I taught them to you because you are a beautiful, vibrant, rich lady living on your own in a world mixed with good and bad. I hoped the lessons I taught you would keep you safe."

Dani saw the way Mo looked at her when her mother had said she was rich. She knew it was time to confess she wasn't the penniless woman she appeared to be. That should be an interesting conversation.

"So, this Ahmed works for you?" her father cut in.

"Yes. He's very good at his job."

"I assume everyone believes Danielle is safer here than in my compound in Italy, since she is still here. I'd like to know why."

Dani was about to answer her father when Ahmed walked confidently into the room in his black slacks and matching dress shirt left open at the collar.

"Simple. They can get into your compound just as easily as they can get her here. However, if she's here, she has me, my team, an FBI agent, a group of retired special forces, and a very protective town all looking out for her."

"So what's the plan? Because I have a few ideas myself." That was her mother for you, always thinking.

# Chapter Fourteen

Mo introduced Ahmed to her parents and sat back down, placing his hand on her knee. Dani caught the glare from her father and was pretty proud when Mo just smiled. Most men were scared of her father, but Mo seemed to like his overprotective side.

"Ahmed, please fill us in on what you've learned today," Dani said. She hoped there would be some kind of information they could use to capture Chad and bring down the rest of the corrupt group.

"For a trained member of the government, Edwards was pathetic. It took only eight minutes to break him. He told us about Assistant Director Pottinger and the judges involved. It appears the vice mayor, Jarred Felting, is nothing but a follower.

"Edwards said his only involvement with GTH was stopping by to pick up some envelopes for Pottinger. It's not enough to tie GTH into the takedown. Cole wants to find some connection before taking them all down. We have to wait for Kenna to get back from her honeymoon and hope she remembers enough of the faces to tie them all together. However, we did build on some more of the intelligence Danielle had discovered in New York. The group is very nervous about Chad. They think he's had a mental breakdown. Instead of doing as he was ordered and killing Kenna, he has been toying with her. Edwards told me that Chad might be eliminated and replaced soon. He also admitted that Judge LeMaster was involved in hiding the 9-1-1 tape. We'll start looking into that now."

"I hate to hash this all out again, but why exactly do you need to bring down the whole group of them?" Mary asked.

"First, we don't have a body. There is no physical evidence of a crime. Cole has enough to arrest Chad, but not the others. There are some petty crimes we've uncovered, like lying on the affidavit for Kenna and Dani's warrants, but Edwards is now in our custody. We have his testimony that certain judges can be bought, but we have to find actual evidence of it. Just like with Whitney. We have her testimony against Chad and her father, but we need evidence. Cole has a man working on the inside searching for that evidence. Until we have indisputable evidence, going forward would scare them into destroying all evidence. That's why we're going to be holding Edwards on ice along with Whitney. Cole is going to put forth a report about Edwards being killed in a gas station robbery. He ran Edwards's credit cards to match his actions while in Kentucky."

"So, what does Danielle do now? How much longer does she have to wait until this is over?" Her mother sounded so worried that Dani didn't know how she could handle the guilt. Between her mother and father worrying about her and Kenna trying to take the blame for it all, this whole ordeal was affecting too many lives.

"She's doing just what she's supposed to do. She's living her life out in the open. We have someone following her constantly to make sure there are no tails or no more surprises from those like Edwards. We're hoping someone will step into our trap, someone like Chad, and we can take them down."

"I do not like this, Bella. I do not like it one bit." Her father shook his head. "However, it seems you're doing everything you can to stay safe. To make sure, your mother and I'll be staying for a while. I have placed my brother in charge of the winery for the next month."

"You and your wife are more than welcome to stay here if you would like," Mo told her parents.

She already knew the answer. There was no way in hell her father would allow her to stay in this house with Mo while no commitment had been made. It didn't matter she was a grown woman. When it came to the men in Danielle's life, her father was the greatest protector she'd ever seen.

"Thank you for the kind offer. However, it's my belief an unmarried woman shouldn't be spending the night with a man. Bella, we've reserved a room where you are staying."

Dani tried not to roll her eyes. She was twenty-seven, not seventeen! But, in her father's eyes she'd always be six years old with long pigtails tied in bows.

"It is such a beautiful bed and breakfast and Miss Rose is just wonderful," her mother praised.

"I will be happy to drive you back to Miss Lily's then. Dani, why don't you show your mother the garden? I want to discuss your father's next donation to my charity." Mo gave her knee a little squeeze and then stood up, holding out his hand to help her up.

Her mother rose and held out her hand for her to take. "I would love to see it. If it is nearly as beautiful as your house, then I am sure I'll enjoy it and be immensely jealous."

Dani took her mother's hand and cast one last questioning glance to Mo before walking out. "I wonder what that was all about."

"Bella, really? I didn't think you were so clueless. The man is obviously in love with you, as he should be," her mother said, causing Dani to blush. "And you are obviously just as in love with him as I am with your father. I'm very happy for you. It is what your father and I always wanted for you."

"Sure didn't look like Papa was happy."

"Well, you have to admit it wasn't the first meeting anyone pictured. Hands, mouths, and other body parts all engaged... not what a father wants to see. I, on the other hand, think it goes to show you will have a very happy marriage. Oh! Look at those roses!"

"Wait, Mama. Who said anything about marriage?" But her mother was already lost in the rows of red, white, pink, and yellow roses.

Dani and her mother were sitting on a stone bench looking at the ornate racehorse fountain when she saw Mo walking toward them. He smiled and waved to them.

"It looks like good news then. I am glad we are staying. I'll meet you at the car. And, Bella, don't take too long. Your father may be appeased right now, but it won't last if you disappear for an extended period of time."

She nodded even though she was feeling pretty stupid. She was missing one big piece of this puzzle. Her mother hugged Mo and he pointed her toward the house.

"How was your meeting with my father?"

"Good."

"Good. That's it?"

"Yes, that's it. Did you enjoy the garden with your mother?" She nodded and looked back to the fountain. "After just two nights together, I'm already missing you in my bed tonight. I have gotten attached to sleeping with you."

"Me, too," she smiled. She snuggled into his chest when he put his arm around her shoulder. It really was quite amazing how fast she fell into a pattern of expectations with him. She, too, had expected to spend the rest of her nights with him. The thought of sleeping alone in her big bed at Miss Lily's saddened her.

"I have never had to do this, but let me into Miss Lily's tonight and I'll leave early in the morning."

"Are you serious? You'd sneak into the house as if you were a teenage boy?"

"I don't really know what that means, but yes."

"Okay," she smiled. Being in love was so much fun. "When facing the house, my room is the last window on the left on the second floor. There's a huge tree that should be easy for you to climb."

"You expect me to climb to your window? I mean, you're worth it, but I have never climbed anywhere." Mo's look of shock caused Dani to laugh. She pushed back a piece of his black hair that had fallen over his eye and quickly kissed his lips as she smiled at him. "Fine, I will do it. As soon as you turn off your light, I will start climbing up. The window just better be unlocked." Mo stood up and held out his hand. She took it and they laughed about the lengths they'd go through for love as they made their way to the limousine waiting to take them to Miss Lily's.

Dani slipped off her bra and panties and pulled on an old button-up shirt. She brushed her teeth and checked her hair before flipping off the lights in her room. She went over to the window and opened it. She looked out into the perfectly manicured yard but didn't see Mo. It had been an hour since he dropped them off and said his goodbyes.

She was about to give up hope when she saw him walking across the front yard as if he was on his way to a business meeting. He sure didn't know the meaning of the word *sneak*. He stopped at the base of the tree and smiled up at her. Grabbing a low-hanging branch, he easily pulled himself up and climbed to her window.

"Are you sure you never climbed a tree before?"

"I practiced in the park while I waited. It's a lot of fun! We don't have trees like this in Rahmi." He walked across the limb and easily stepped onto the window seat. "If I get to see you dressed like that, I will climb a tree every night. Now, I believe you told me earlier this evening that there were some things you wanted to do." Mo pulled his shirt over his head and tossed it onto the window seat. He moved to the bed and sat down, kicking off his shoes. "I am all yours, love." He leaned back on his elbows and Dani stared at his muscled chest and flat, sculpted stomach.

Oh, the things she wanted to do! Her eyes traveled upward to his face and she saw his amber eyes darken. She raised her fingers to the top of her shirt and unbuttoned it. She enjoyed the rush of seeing his eyes glued to her as she undid button after button. Her shirt parted and she shrugged her shoulders, causing the shirt to fall to the floor. She took a deep breath and stepped toward him.

Dani woke up in the predawn morning. She was warm and completely relaxed. But she thought she had heard something. There it was again. There was noise above her. Her parents were already up!

"Mo!" She whispered. When he didn't respond, she rolled over in his arms and shook him. "Mo, you need to wake up."

"Hmm. It's still dark out, love. Go back to bed."

"Mo, you have to leave. My parents are on European time, they are already up."

Mo shot up in bed and scrambled out, not bothering to cover up. He flashed a smile as he walked around the room picking up his clothing.

"I guess this means I get to make my exit via the tree. I was really hoping for the door." He leaned out the window and tossed his shoes out. "I'll see you for dinner tonight. Ahmed said he had some problems fitting in at your office, so the Davies brothers will be in charge of your safety inside the office. When they are unavailable, Cole will post FBI outside your office for surveillance. Marshall will go over the schedule with you today." He walked over to the bed and kissed her goodbye. "Be careful. I love you."

She crawled out of bed and watched as he worked his way down to the ground. He was about to pick up his shoes when he jumped back and crashed into the tree trunk. Peering over the windowsill, Dani saw Miss Lily standing on the edge of the porch with a hose in her hand. When Mo stepped away from the tree, she saw that he was soaking wet. Dani tried not to laugh and leaned further out the window to hear the conversation.

"Good morning, Miss Lily." Mo smiled and bent down for his shoes.

"Good morning, Mohtadi. So sorry I sprayed you. I always get up and water my plants before the hot sun can wilt them. What a surprise to see you dangling out of my tree. I trust that I'll not have you dangling in my trees every morning? After all, what would the neighbors think?"

She saw Mo smile as he slipped on his shoes. "No, ma'am. Now that I know you're awake, I will just use the front door." Dani laughed when she saw Mo jerk back as Miss Lily sprayed him again. Mo chuckled and shook his head, sending water drops flying off. He tucked his wet pieces of hair behind his ears before giving Miss Lily a little wink. He waved good-bye to Miss Lily and walked down the street to where his car was parked.

Dani got dressed and had breakfast with her parents. They were planning on sightseeing and she had walked to work with Ahmed's car driving slowly behind her. Signs were being put up all around town for the county fair that ran from Friday through Sunday. She didn't even know if there was a county fair in New York. But it was one of the social events of the year in Keeneston. There were beauty pageants ranging from baby to seniors. Every contestant got a picture in the weekly gossip rag/newspaper. There were concerts, tractor pulls, pig wrestling matches, and 4-H livestock shows. It sounded so bizarre that she couldn't wait to go.

She opened the door to the office and noticed Tammy staring off at the corner of the room. Dani followed her gaze and found Miles reading *Field and Stream* while Marshall read the *Keeneston Journal*.

"Morning, guys. What brings both of you to the office today?"

"Good morning, Dani. We hoped you'd come in early enough for a quick self-defense review. Marshall will stay here for the rest of the day, but tomorrow we're both tied up at the fair. We'll make sure FBI is stationed outside, though. Cole has informed the agents in the Lexington office that Edwards had died. He also said it was Edwards who had issued the phony call regarding Dani and Kenna. So you won't have any worries about them arresting you," Miles told her.

"Thank you both. I feel so much better knowing you're out here. I know it must be boring to sit out here doing nothing."

"I'm glad. We'll be here as much as we can. Let us show you some more moves for the times when we aren't around. Miles and I'll demonstrate and then you try them. Okay?"

She nodded and moved back when Miles and Marshall strode to the center of the lobby. Dani took a quick look and saw Tammy had taken a seat on her desk, her feet dangling over the front as she smiled at the men.

Miles moved behind Marshall. He reached around Marshall's neck and put him in a headlock. "This is a traditional attack move. A person will come up from behind you and slip his arm across your neck. The pressure will panic most people. You have to remember that most attackers don't know how to do this move properly. If you keep calm, then you'll be able to breathe. Always slip your fingers between his arm and your neck, but don't try to claw at his arm or he'll tighten it. With your fingers there, it makes it difficult to completely cut off the air. Watch."

Miles demonstrated on Marshall and then on her. "That's right, just apply gentle, steady pressure with your fingers. Keep calm. Breathe through your nose. Good," Marshall told her as Miles let go and she took a big gasp for air. She was able to breathe but only a little. Still, a little was better than nothing.

"If you're in this type of situation, you have two options. The first is to fight immediately, and if there's a weapon involved, it's best to do that. If there's a car involved, you want to fight with everything you have. If they get you into that car, your chance of survival plummets. However, if he has you in an improper headlock," Miles put her in another headlock, but this time it felt different. If she just lowered her head, the lock was more around her jaw than her throat. "Then you can try to talk your way out of it or stall until help comes. I'm usually in favor of attacking instantly, but sometimes you need a moment to calm down and take in your surroundings before knowing how to act," Miles explained.

Miles went back to Marshall and put him in another lock. "To get out of the lock, there are two things you can do. First, you're tall and can reach back with both hands and place them on his ears. Your thumbs will be in his face. You can then gouge the eyes. To fully escape, hang on and pull his head sideways. He'll follow." Miles showed her how to do it and then she tried. It was clumsy and she could see if she was too slow her attacker could pick up on it.

"The next is all about leverage. If you move your left leg behind his right leg and then hit him with your left elbow to his midsection, you can knock him down. See how I hit, then push with my arm at his midsection, causing Marshall to trip over the leg I placed behind him? Come on, you try it."

Dani tried over and over again. By the fifth time, she had Marshall down on the ground in one movement.

"That is so cool! Can I try it?" Tammy jumped up and stood in front of Miles. Wrapping his arm around her, he instructed her on what to do.

"Okay, go."

"No, this is just fine like this." Tammy sighed and laid her head back against Miles's chest.

"Tammy! You're just as bad as Henry, and that is not a compliment. Now kick his butt!" Dani chided her while trying not to laugh. Tammy did the move and Miles went to the ground.

"So, is there anything we can do down here together?" Tammy asked as she leaned over Miles.

"Sorry, kid. You're a little too young for me. However, my brother Pierce should be just perfect for you," Miles chuckled before standing up.

"Pierce? I haven't seen him since high school. I don't mean to sound rude, but he's not really my type." She turned to Dani and explained. "He was so skinny. All knees and elbows. He had braces with white and blue bands and he played in the band. He was a band geek! Not to mention president of the Future Farmers of America."

Miles and Marshall burst out laughing.

"What? I know he's your brother, but he's a geek!"

"Nothing. It'll be better if it's a surprise," Miles said with a huge smile. He then said good-bye to her and Dani and headed out.

Dani went to the front door and flipped the Closed sign to Open and waited for the inevitable line of women to come. It didn't help that Marshall was wearing the tightest black t-shirt she'd ever seen, or that he was opening the door and complimenting all the women who came in. Henry didn't care, though. He was happy as a pig in mud with an office full of desperate women.

She turned on her computer and pulled up the legal research site. She still needed to find some case law on the adoption case she was working. The man and woman who wanted to adopt the baby were foster parents. They had gotten a call from the hospital explaining that baby Emma had been abandoned by her birth mother. Eight months had gone by and they decided to adopt the little girl. After meeting with the social worker, the drugged-out mother showed up demanding they turn the baby over to her. Dani started the program and searched the relevant statutes and started reading cases. She looked up when she heard someone walk into the office.

"Hey, Danielle. How about some lunch?" Henry walked into the office and sat down in one of her chairs.

"Sorry, Henry, I have about ten more cases to read and then I have an early dinner with my parents."

"Wow! Those are really nice shoes, wanna fu..."

"Henry! If I passed on lunch, then do you really think I'd have sex with you because you compliment the shoes you can't even see?" She rolled her eyes. "Go take one of those women drooling over Marshall. You can't be above going after the women he rejected."

"Good point!" Henry jumped up and headed for the front of the building.

Dani found case law supporting the adoption and highlighted it. She laid it on Kenna's desk and rolled her head, stretching her neck. She heard the bell tinkle and heard Tammy flittering. It was either another Davies boy or Mo had come to pick her up. Mo walked around the corner and Dani had to stop herself from trying out Henry's line about shoes. Mo looked delectable in a dark brown suit and ivory dress shirt.

"Good afternoon, love." Mo wrapped her up in a hug and dipped her back for a kiss. "Ready to see me on the hot seat with your parents again?"

"At least my father isn't yelling at you to get your hands off me anymore." She laughed as she grabbed her purse and shut down her computer. "I was thinking about going to the fair this weekend. Would you like to go with me? I'd love to see you wrestle a pig!"

"Why would I wrestle a pig?"

"To win me a prize, of course! Tammy says they slick a pig up and if you catch it, then you win a prize."

"I love you, but I don't know if I love you enough to chase after a slicked-up pig. Sorry, love, but I would love to accompany you. It might be fun to see you catch a pig and win me a prize!" He walked her outside and waited as she locked the front door. "Marshall left when I got here. Did he tell you the FBI will be here tomorrow to look after you?"

"Yes. Miles told me that Cole passed the story off as Edwards's forging the documents from Pottinger. And that they wanted to keep an eye on me just to make sure I was safe from other threats of any kind." She waved to Roger Burns as he slowly made his way down the street toward the Blossom Cafe. A horn blew and she turned to wave at one of Kenna's clients as they drove by. She was amazed at how fast Keeneston had turned into her home.

"I guess you saw Miss Lily ambush me this morning."

"Yes. That was pretty funny. I also noticed she didn't tell my parents about it."

"So, I'll see you tonight then."

"Same place, same time."

She and Mo walked up the stairs and into Miss Lily's house.

Delicious smells were coming from the dining room where she found her parents. "*Ciao, il mio amore.*" Her father said in Italian as he stood to envelop her in a hug.

"Hello, Papa, Mama. Did you have a nice day?"

"Oh, it was wonderful. We took a bourbon-tasting tour and traveled to all of the local distilleries," her mother told her when she hugged Dani. "I've calmed your father, so don't worry," her mother whispered as the men shook hands. Dani and Mo sat down at the round table and she felt like she was back home in Italy.

Conversation flowed, food was passed, polite arguments were had, and politics debated. It was a typical dinner for her family. She could tell that Mo was taken aback at first, but he soon got into a debate with her father over Italian opera. He surprised her by making the argument for Handel as one of the most influential Italian composers, despite being born in Germany.

"Mo! I didn't know you spoke Italian."

"Of course he does, Bella. He has always spoken to me in Italian when we discuss the foundation." Her father went back to his debate with Mo and her mother gave her a wink. Her father was warming up to the man she loved and nothing could be more important.

They talked about opera, books, his racing stable, and charity. They talked about the rich history of her father's vineyard and how it had been in the family for almost three hundred years. Her father was the current president and, being the patriarch, lived at the property. His brother and sister also helped run the operation. Dani's uncle was going to retire soon and her cousin, Franco, would be taking over for him.

Dani paused mid-bite when she heard a pot crash in the kitchen. She noticed everyone turned and looked at the swinging door when they heard Miss Lily shout, "Get! Get out of here right now!" The swinging door pushed open and Dani caught sight of a orange blur streaking into the dining room. Miss Lily came running through the door next, with her broom in hand. Brutus darted across the room and leapt into Dani's lap.

"Brutus, what have you done?" Before she could find out, Miss Lily's broom smacked him on the head. Dani heard the low growl, but it sounded muffled. She looked closer and saw a little tail hanging out of his mouth. "Oh, gross!" Dani jumped up, dropping Brutus to the ground.

"Don't give me that evil look! You have a mouse in your mouth! Get outside, now!" Miss Lily went to open the front door and found herself in a staring contest with a cat. That is, until Miss Lily smacked his rump with the broom again. Brutus gave her the cat eye, so she smacked him again. "This, this, cat destroyed a pot filled with heavy cream when he decided his little treat would go down nice with a drink. He tipped it over and then set the mouse down to lap up the cream. When I tried to sweep him and his treat outside, he growled at me and darted in here."

"Come on, Brutus. Outside." Brutus just stared at her. She placed her hands on her hips and decided to get tough. "Fine. No more dinners over at Mo's." Dani raised her eyebrow and stared him down. She heard the contained laughter at the table and knew she looked ridiculous negotiating with a cat. But she felt a surge of satisfaction when Brutus finally blinked. He stood up, tossed his head back, and slowly swaggered out of the house.

After dessert and wine from the De Luca winery, the men retired to the front porch to smoke cigars. Dani and her mother sat on the comfortable white-and-yellow-striped sofa in the sitting room. She could hear her father and Mo laughing outside and smiled.

"It's nice, isn't it?"

"What is, Mama?"

"To find the man you want to spend the rest of your life with."

"It is. But it's happening so fast, Mama. I have only known him two weeks." Dani shared the internal fear she had been struggling with to her mother. She was scared he'd change his mind about her after knowing her for so little time. Numerous "what ifs" kept popping into her head. What if he didn't like that she wore socks to bed on cold nights? What if he didn't like that she'd eat her breakfast over the sink when she was in a hurry?

"Bella, do you not remember the story of how I met your father?"

"Of course I do. You met in Aspen when you were skiing."

"Oh, there's so much more. I had just competed in the Lake Placid Olympics and finished fourth in downhill. I missed out on medaling by one hundredth of a second. Upset, I decided to head to Aspen to relax and ski some. It was my first day there. I was on my second run of the day when I went flying by a group of six men. At the bottom of the hill, I took off my skis and went to get a drink. A handsome man approached me at the coffee shop. I recognized him as one of the group I passed. He introduced himself as Tony. He told me that he and his cousins were visiting for the week and asked if he could buy me a cup of coffee. He brought it back to the table and we have been inseparable ever since. You talk about things moving fast. We were engaged before we left Aspen at the end of the week."

Her mother continued. "Your grandfather was furious. He made your father look like a teddy bear. He threatened him with a bear trap! But it didn't matter to me, and eventually your grandfather saw that. Just like your father, Grandpa accepted it in the end. Now your father is the son Grandpa never had. We stayed at your grandfather's long enough to get married in my church and pack. Bella, when you talk of fears and not knowing each other long enough, all I can do is tell you that time is inconsequential when dealing with matters of the heart. You will find that if you love a person, truly love him, then you will love all of his faults just as much as all of his assets. I have been married to your father for twenty-nine years and I still find things out about him that I didn't know before. That's the wonderful part of marriage, Bella."

Her mother patted her leg and stood up as her father and Mo walked inside. "Tony, let's go to bed and leave these young ones to their night." With a wink, her mother steered her father upstairs to their third-floor room.

"I think your mother has the right idea. Think we can sneak up without Miss Lily seeing us?" Mo held out his hand and she placed it in his. He gave it a little squeeze and peeked in the door. "Shh. She's in the kitchen. Come on."

She stood up, stifled a laugh, and let Mo lead her upstairs. He opened her bedroom door and they quickly jumped inside when they heard Miss Lily in the foyer. As soon as the door was closed, his hands were on her body. He ran his fingers up and down her back.

"I have wanted to touch you all over since I picked you up at the office today." He reached down and pulled off her shirt. He slid his hands up to her breasts and cupped them before pulling down the straps of her bra. He kissed her hard and fast before he moved his lips to her neck. "Even more, I have wanted you naked."

"I think that can be arranged."

# Chapter Fifteen

Dani couldn't stop the extra bounce in her step any more than she could keep the smile off her face. She should be exhausted. Instead, the hours of lovemaking left her feeling giddy. They had made love into the night and then once again at dawn.

She pulled open the door to her office and found Henry practicing his golf swing. Tammy was behind the desk making faces as he tried to swing at a crumpled ball of paper.

"Should I even ask?"

"No."

"Yes." Tammy laughed and Henry looked embarrassed. "See, Henry signed up for the Chamber of Commerce Golf Scramble at the fair today. What he failed to think through is that he has never played golf!" Tammy laughed again when Henry swung and missed again. "Strike three! You're out!"

"Geez, Tammy, way to be supportive." Dani walked over to Henry and took the club out of his hand. "Watch. Fingers laced. Stand straight, but not too rigid. Eyes on the ball. Pull back. Swing." She demonstrated and handed the club back to Henry.

"Maybe if you were more hands-on in showing me..."

"You're persistent, I'll give you that."

"Well, can I get a kiss for luck?"

"No! Now get out of here, Henry." Dani laughed as she watched Henry pick up his clubs and stagger out the door.

"He's a mess," Dani joked.

"I know. Don't forget that I have to work the bake sale for Saint Frances Church this afternoon."

"Yes. I remember." The ringing phone cut off the conversation before Dani could ask when Tammy was going to head out. She walked into her office, put her purse down behind the desk, and turned on her computer.

She had a list of things to look up for Kenna before court on Monday. She looked into criminal statutes and case law for most of the morning. The phone and walk-ins kept Tammy busy nonstop. At noon, Dani grabbed a frozen lunch and quickly returned to her work. The work took twice as long to complete since she kept stopping to think about Mo. She was making a list of all the things she wanted to do with him this weekend. She was also thinking she needed to remember her camera for the fair. She didn't know how she was going to do it, but she wanted a picture of him wrestling an oily pig. Oh, what his father would do if he saw that!

"Knock-knock."

"Hmm?"

"I want to know what, or should I say who, you were thinking about to get such a look on your face." Tammy walked into the room and put a hip up on the corner of her desk.

"I'll never tell. Are you heading out now?"

"Yup. Going to sell brownies, cookies, and lemonade. Maybe some hottie will have a sweet tooth."

"Good luck with that."

"Are you going to be here much longer?" Dani looked down at the note Kenna left and sighed. She'd been daydreaming too much.

"Unfortunately. I can probably finish in an hour."

"Okay. I'll put the Closed sign up and lock the front door so no one will bother you. Most people are making their way to the fair now anyway. Have a good time this weekend."

Dani watched Tammy jump off the desk and skip out the door. She heard the front door open, close, and then the lock being thrown. She scanned over Kenna's note and saw the last law that she needed to research. She didn't bother to look up when she heard the bolt being unlocked or the tinkle of the bell over the door.

"What did you forget, Tammy?"

"One thing I can never forget is you."

Dani's head shot up and all of the blood drained from her face. Black splotches appeared in front of her eyes and danced around. "Chad," she whispered. She started to move to grab her gun hidden away in her purse, but Chad was faster. He dove over the desk, crashed into her, and knocked her to the floor. His legs hit her computer and sent it crashing to the ground. Her purse flew out of her hands and landed to the side of the desk.

She couldn't breathe. When he landed on her, he knocked the wind out of her. Her head felt like it was split in two when it cracked against the floor. She lashed out with her hands in panic as she tried to get some air into her lungs. She couldn't tear her eyes away from his face. He looked like he had lost a lot of weight and his spray tan had worn off. But the unmistakable glint of evil still shown in his eyes. His mouth curved up in a smile. He loved watching her fight him.

He shifted so he was straddling her. He sat on her stomach and smiled as his hands closed around her throat. Dani stopped clawing at his hands and extended her first two fingers together. She jabbed as hard as she could into the base of his throat. Chad fell back grasping his throat and coughing to catch his breath. Dani wriggled out from under him and hit the wall. Using it as a support, she stood up and grabbed the nearest object she could find. She threw a framed picture at him. He deflected it to the side and glass shattered all around him.

He stood between her and the door. She had to make it around him and her desk to be able to get out of the room. She took a deep breath and pushed off the wall, trying to make a dash to the door.

Chad lunged forward from where he sat on his knees. She felt his hand clamp down on her ankle. She fell forward and the left side of her head hit the corner of her desk. Her teeth broke through the inside of her lip as she landed hard on the floor.

"You stupid bitch! Do you really think I'd let you escape?" he laughed.

Dani pulled back her free left leg and looked back at him. He was smiling again. Kicking as hard as she could, she hit him right in the mouth. Blood started pouring out of his mouth where she split his lip. His grip loosened on her leg and she tried to crawl free. Chad just laughed again. The sound was pure evil. Her hair stood on end as she lost her focus and blind panic took over.

He laughed again as he stood up. She made it to her knees before he struck again. Her head was jerked back. His hand tangled in her hair as he pulled with all his strength. She fell backwards and landed against his legs. Tears streaked her face as she tasted blood pooling in her mouth. She felt his arm slide across her throat and squeeze. She instinctively lowered her chin and managed a breath of air. She took another gasp of air and focused. Miles had held her the same way and shown her how to get out of it. Chad had slipped his arm around her throat too high and she was able to block some of the pressure to her throat.

"It's just too bad Kenna isn't here to enjoy this with us," Chad said as his lips brushed against her ear.

"Why does Bob want me killed? I didn't see anything." Dani spat out a mouthful of blood.

"You saw Kenna and me. And Kenna told you about what she saw. You're a loose end. An end I'm going to enjoy tying up." He pressed up against her back as he squeezed her breast hard. She sucked in a deep breath and reminded herself to stay calm. It was getting harder and harder to do, though. She could feel the panic turning her stomach into a hurricane and clawing its way upward.

"What happened to the girl?"

"Which one?"

"You mean more than one girl has been killed by you and Bob?" She just had to keep him talking. Miles said the FBI was outside. Where were they?

"One for every poker game." The panic burst through. She clawed at Chad's arm and kicked for all the she was worth. He pulled his arm tight and she choked and gasped for breath. "I like it when you're feisty. It'll make what comes next even more fun."

"What happened to the women? How have they not been found?" She shoved the panic down and remembered Miles had told her to breathe and look around for her options to defend herself. During the struggle, her purse had overturned and was about eight feet in front of her. If she could just get to it, she might make it out alive.

"They'll never be found. Senator Bruce's men take the bodies out to some swampland that Bob owns outside the city and dumps them. It's a little too far for me to take you to join them, but I'm sure I'll find a nice abandoned farm to bury you on."

Dani took as deep a breath as possible. She kept her eyes on her bag. Chad moved his mouth along her ear and Dani made her move. In one smooth motion, she moved her leg behind his and shoved with all her might while twisting away. Chad was pushed backwards to the ground as his knee collapsed. She jumped away from him and dove forward. Her hand slid into the purse. She felt him getting up as she scrambled for the gun. Panic caused her vision to narrow as her hand kept coming up empty. Chad laughed and her panic literally blinded her. Finally, her hand felt the cold, hard steel of her gun. She wrapped her hand around it, switched off the safety, and pulled the gun out. She was too panicked to see where she shot. She kept shooting until the magazine was empty.

She didn't hear the glass shattering or the footsteps pounding down the hall. She just kept pulling the trigger over and over until a gentle hand pushed the gun down and slowly took it out of her hands. She blinked through the blood and tears streaming down her face and looked into the worried eyes of Dinky.

"Dinky!" She rasped out and collapsed into him. "Is he dead?"

"Yes. Come on, let's get you out of here." Dinky picked her up and carried her to the lobby.

"Now I really will have to come up with a new nickname for you."

Dani felt Dinky lay her down on the leather sofa in the lobby. She turned her head away from her office and stared at the brown leather cushions on the couch. She heard Dinky radio in for help. Her body started shaking and she was so focused on trying to stop it that she jumped when Dinky's hand touched her shoulder.

"Are you okay, Dani? Let me look at the cut on your head."

"Is he dead?" She knew she had already asked that, but she couldn't get the image of a bloody Chad staggering out from the office with a gun drawn. Or worse, if he had simply vanished. She didn't think she could handle looking over her shoulder for the rest of her life. "Please, just go make sure he's still there and he's still dead." Her body shivered and she curled up in a ball to keep warm.

"Dani, I'm sure he's dead. But I'll go look again if it'll make you feel better."

"Please, Dinky. I just need you to make sure he's really dead." She heard Dinky stand up and walk into her office. Less than a minute later, she heard footsteps come back. She knew it was Dinky, but her body broke out in sweat. She couldn't stop this irrational feeling that Chad was still coming to kill her. She clawed at the couch trying to hide in it.

"Dani. It's just me. It's okay. I can tell you he's definitely dead." Her heart slowed down and she released her death grip on the couch. She tensed again when she heard glass crunching by the door.

"Dammit, Dinky. You should've waited for me. What happened? Is she okay?" Noodle walked through the broken glass door and flipped the deadbolt.

"She's in shock. She also took a nasty hit to the head. Chad Taylor is back in her office with ten rounds in him. What about the FBI agents?"

"They're dead. Each took a shot to the head. Red is out there placing all the calls."

"Has he called Agent Parker?"

"Yes. He's on his way. He told us not to call the coroner or ambulance until he gets here. I'll call him and let him know Miss De Luca is injured and Chad is dead." He turned and she heard him walk toward her. "Miss De Luca? Agent Parker is on his way. I'll get an EMT here now to look at your head. How are you feeling?"

Dani closed her eyes. She didn't want to talk to any of them. She just wanted to sleep. Her eyes popped open when she felt someone grab her shoulder. She screamed and tried to jump away.

"Danielle. Danielle. Shhh. It's just me, Noodle. You're injured, Miss De Luca. I don't want you falling asleep until the medics can look at you. They are on their way. Just keep your eyes open. Can you do that for me?"

She nodded but groaned at the pain shooting through her head. She felt Noodle brush her hair back and turn to Dinky. "Go back to the kitchen and see if you can find a towel. She's losing a lot of blood."

"Those men are dead because of me." Tears welled in her eyes and started cascading down her face.

"What men?" Noodle asked as he gently began to brush back her hair and examine her wound.

"The FBI agents. And, Noodle, there were so many more women. All those poor girls. But I know where they are. I know and I can't get their pictures out of my head. Those faceless victims tossed aside like garbage." She felt the coolness of the leather as she hid her face in the leather and cried for those poor women and for the FBI agents and their families.

"Shh. It's okay. It'll be all right," she heard him whisper.

She jerked her head back when she felt a cold pack placed on her head. "What is that?"

"Some frozen vegetables Dinky found in the freezer. I want to slow down the bleeding. Head wounds can be dangerous if the bleeding isn't controlled. How did you get this gash on your head?"

"I tried to escape and he grabbed my ankle. I fell forward and my head hit the corner of my desk."

Noodle was pressing the veggies wrapped in a washcloth hard against her head when she heard sirens and shouts coming from the street. As if they were three avenging angels with white halos and Easy Spirit wings, the Rose sisters descended on the office. They surrounded Dani, pushing Dinky and Noodle out of the way. In hushed tones, they worked, never asking Dani a question. Her body, once racked with chills, started to warm as Lily wrapped her in a heavy patchwork quilt. A cup of hot tea was placed to her lips and Violet gently urged her to drink. Daisy raised her head slightly and a pillow was placed under her. She had to remember to tell Kenna that she was right—the Roses were fairy godmothers.

Dani's head continued to feel as if it were about to explode and she couldn't stop crying. But, as the Roses surrounded her and police flooded the office, she felt safe. At least the body shaking chills had stopped.

"It's okay, child. The ambulance will be here soon. They are coming from Lexington. Oh, bless your heart, you'll be okay. It'll take a while, but you'll start feeling better soon. I called your parents and Mo. They'll be here soon. Just take a sip of tea, dear." Lily told her as a teacup was pressed to her lips again. She took a sip and coughed as she felt liquor burn and then soothe her sore throat.

"Lily Rae! Please tell me you did not just give this child some bourbon in that tea."

"Of course I did, Daisy Mae! After what she's been through, a good shot of bourbon will be a great help. Look at those bruises along her neck." Dani felt her shirt pushed away and heard the gasps from Daisy and Violet.

"Well, don't just sit there, Lily Rae, pour some more of that in the tea while those officers aren't looking." Dani wanted to laugh at Miss Violet, but a sob came out instead. Tears rolled down her face, this time in thanksgiving.

"Okay. Everyone, I need this area cleared. If you are nonessential personnel, please head outside to control the crowd. Thank you." She heard Cole usher people out and walk over to her. "How are you doing, Dani?"

"I don't know," she rasped out. She felt as if she were outside her own body, floating above it. The sounds from the street seemed far away. She had kept her back to the office so she only caught glimpses of the people coming and going.

"I know this is hard, but I need to know what happened." Cole stepped past the protective barrier the Rose sisters had put up, placed his hand on her shoulder, and turned her toward him. "It's really important, Dani."

"I know it is." She opened her eyes and saw Cole's blurry figure through her tears. She tried to sit up, but she felt dizzy and a sharp pain played pinball in her head.

"Danielle! Get out of my way. Danielle!"

"Mo!" She held out her hand and relief washed over her when he grabbed it. His face was pale and drawn. He touched the gash on her head and cursed in multiple languages. She only caught the ones in English and Italian, but their creativity tugged a smile out of her lips. "I'm okay, Mo. Just got the sense knocked out of me."

"Mo, the EMTs are on the way. Before they get here and try to take her to the hospital, I need her to tell me what happened," Cole told him. When Mo nodded his understanding, Ahmed stepped up next to Cole and whispered to him.

"What is it, Ahmed?" Dani said as she took another sip of the tea to help keep her voice.

"If you're up to it, we can get a better description of what happened if you show us. I'll cover the body. Do you think you're up to it?"

"I'll need help standing."

While Mo helped her up, the Rose sisters clucked and scolded Cole and Ahmed. Her head spun so violently that she thought she'd throw up. She took in a couple of deep breaths and waited for the worst of the nausea to stop. Ahmed, having escaped the lectures of the Roses, came to her other side.

"I'm sorry, Danielle. But you'll remember more and we'll have to ask fewer questions if you can walk us through it." He and Mo guided her through the lobby. Before she could make it through the archway, she heard her father outside yelling in Italian at an officer.

"Cole. Have the officers let her parents in. I am sure Paige will be here soon. They'll want to see her to make sure she's okay."

Cole agreed and went off to leave orders on who to allow into the office.

"It's okay, love. You're safe. I know this will be hard, but I will be right here with you. I will never leave your side. Ever."

"Oh, Bella!" Her mother raced across the room with her father close behind.

"It's okay, Mama, Papa. I'm alright."

"You told me she was safe. What happened? How did he get to her?" Her father was livid. He yelled at Ahmed as if he were responsible for what happened.

"Papa! It's not his fault. Chad killed the two FBI agents who were watching me." Tears welled again in her eyes. How could she possible have any more tears in her?

"Tony. Two families lost their loved ones while we still have ours. Let us thank God that we do not share their sorrow." Her mother had superpowers. When she placed her hand gently on her husband's arm, Dani could see her father's blood pressure drop.

"You're right, my dear, as always." He kissed her mother and then placed a soft kiss on Dani's cheek. "Do you want us to go with you?" he nodded to her office.

"No, Papa. Mo and Ahmed will go with me. Let me just get this over with."

Dani forced her legs forward. Her vision focused on the door and everything else in the world dropped away. Soon, the only sound she heard was the thumping of her heart as it sped up. Ahmed had thrown a black police blanket over Chad's lifeless body. She told herself to not look at him, but she couldn't tear her eyes away. She pictured the predatory smile on his face as he lay there, waiting to jump up and attack her again. She was about to walk over to the body when Ahmed released her arm and stepped in front of her.

"I know this is difficult, but just keep your eyes on mine." He waited until she raised her eyes from the floor to his. "Now, walk us through what happened."

Dani told them about Tammy leaving and how she thought the noise was just her returning. She told them she was trying to reach for the gun when Chad launched himself across the desk. She could still feel his hands tightening around her throat. Mo took her hand in his and brought it to his lips. She squeezed his hand and continued her account. She told of her attempt for the door and where she hit her head.

"He put me in a headlock after dragging me back by my hair. I realized he didn't have a proper hold on me and I kept thinking the FBI would come to my rescue at any moment. So I started asking him questions. I got it, Cole. I got it."

"Got what? Tell me exactly what was said." Cole placed the recorder closer to her and kept his eyes on hers.

"I asked what happened to the girl, the stripper Kenna saw dragged out of the room in New York. But, he asked me 'Which one?' I asked if he and Bob had killed more than one. He told me that every poker game featured a new girl that would be killed afterwards. I've been there six years and they've been having these poker nights semi-regularly for years now. There are likely dozens of women dead, all because of them."

"What then?"

"I asked how they haven't been found yet, and he told me. He said that Senator Bruce's men would take the bodies out to some swampland that Bob owns and dump them. He then told me he was going to bury me at an abandoned farm. That's when I did what Miles and Marshall taught me and escaped the headlock. My purse was lying beside my desk. My gun was in it. We were standing here, close to the wall. I knocked him down and back. He fell there," she pointed to where he had fallen. "I took a couple of steps and jumped for the bag. I was so panicked that I couldn't find the gun. Chad got up and laughed. I knew he was going to kill me next. I finally felt the gun. I grabbed it, rolled over, and shot him. I know I emptied my clip, but I don't remember if I even hit him."

"You did. You emptied your entire clip into him. You did the right thing, Dani. You also got the evidence we need to bring down the whole ring. I know you don't feel it right now, but you were great. You kept your cool, got the info we needed, and protected yourself. You helped us break this case open on two fronts. Because of what you remembered at the bar, I have agents talking to the bartender right now. I'll let you know what we get from that." Cole turned to the door. "Dinky, you get enough for your report?"

Mo bent down and scooped her up in his arms. He carried her into the lobby where her parents and friends were waiting. "I am taking her back to my house. My private physician will be waiting there for me. I will call each one of you with updates. Mr. and Mrs. De Luca, Ahmed will bring you by later. You may stay at my house if you wish."

"I don't..."

"That sounds like a wonderful plan, Mo. We will see you soon, Bella." Her mother cut her father off and placed a kiss on her cheek.

Mo strode out of the building with Dani in his arms. The police cleared the way to his car and opened the door for him to lay her gently across the backseat. Her eyes closed and she fell into a restless sleep before they had even turned off of Main Street.

# Chapter Sixteen

D ani felt the hands squeezing her throat tighter and tighter. She looked up and into Chad's eyes. He laughed and squeezed tighter. She grabbed her gun and shot over and over. She couldn't look away from him as his dead body stared at her with the crooked and twisted smile still on his face.

"It doesn't end with me. I'll always be looking over my girls."

Dani woke up screaming until her voice gave out. She was drenched in sweat and shaking. Mo grabbed her hands and stopped them from clawing at her throat. She broke out into silent sobs when Mo's arms went around her and pulled her to his chest. The damage from where Chad had choked her stopped her from talking.

"Shh. It's okay, my love. I am here. You're safe. It's just a dream." Mo ran his hand over her hair and brushed it away from her face. "Would you like some ice cream to soothe your throat?"

She nodded, anything to help the feeling of fire dancing in her throat. She had damaged it even more when she screamed from her nightmare. She looked around the room to erase the dark traces of her nightmare. The white curtains were pulled closed and she was tucked into Mo's bed in a large button-up shirt. She took a breath and recognized the smell of Mo's cologne. She looked over to the sitting area and saw a pillow and blanket tossed on one chair, with an open book sitting on the coffee table.

"Your parents are here and Ahmed has an update if you are up to it."

She nodded again. "Thank you," she mouthed.

Mo got up and dialed an extension on his phone. Within minutes, her parents were by her side.

"How are you feeling, Bella?" her mother asked.

"Tired," she mouthed.

"The doctor checked you out and stitched the cut on your head. He also gave you a sedative. You've been asleep for eighteen hours. He said your body needs lots of rest, as does your mind. So you just lay back and rest. We're here if you need us. Mo is being a wonderful host."

"Thank you, Mary. The doctor left you some pain medicine and also a couple of sleeping pills. He warned there would be nightmares and that you might fight sleep."

Dani was more interested in the fact that he had called her mother by her first name than what the doctor said. She looked at her father who was sitting on the other side of the bed, holding Dani's hand. He seemed worried but not angered over the fact that she was spending her recovery time in Mo's room. She thought even a near-death experience wouldn't be enough to convince her father to accept this situation.

"Your mother is right. We're doing fine. You just lay back and rest. Is your throat or head hurting?" When she nodded and pointed to both, her father looked back to Mo. "Why don't you go ahead and give her the medicine? We will let you get some more rest. Just let us know if you need anything."

Her father and mother rose, and each bent to give her a kiss on the forehead before turning to leave. Mo walked over to the nightstand and opened a bottle. He shook out one pill and handed it to her. He opened another bottle and took out a second pill. He opened the mini-fridge built into the nightstand and pulled out a cold bottle of water. He opened the water and handed it to her.

"The first pill is to help with the pain. This second one is to help you sleep."

She had just swallowed the second pill when Ahmed knocked on the door. After Mo called for him to come in, Ahmed opened the door and walked in with a large tray.

"I didn't know which flavor you wanted," he explained as he put a tray down on the bed with four bowls of ice cream on it. "There's chocolate, vanilla, strawberry, and butter pecan." He handed her a spoon and stepped back from the bed.

She dug into the chocolate with a gusto she didn't know she had. Mo and Ahmed stood off to the side of the bed talking while she worked her way through the butter pecan. When they continued to talk, she tapped her spoon against the bowl to get their attention. They both walked over to her. Mo sat on the bed next to her and Ahmed stood at the foot of the bed with his hands behind his back. She raised an eyebrow at him and she could tell from the way he shifted his feet that he was uncomfortable.

"Mo said you had a nightmare." He shifted feet again as she nodded. "Um. Mo wanted me to talk to you about killing someone."

She heard Mo groan and couldn't stop the smile that came to her face. Ahmed looked like he was about to give a group of kids the sex talk. She moved her hand in a circle indicating Ahmed should continue.

"Well, I was only ten, but I remember it well."

"Ten!" she mouthed.

"Long story. Anyway, I remember having horrible nightmares for weeks. They got better every night and eventually they just disappeared. They will for you, too. Just give it time and you will see every night gets a little better. The mind is an amazing thing. It will heal, too. If you ever want to talk about it, just let me know."

"What has happened since yesterday?" she whispered before Ahmed could leave. She took another bite of ice cream and sighed at the instant relief she felt.

"Cole is working hard to uncover all the properties that Bob owns. They are also identifying the men working for Senator Bruce with Whitney's help. Dave is supplying leads to the FBI on everything he knows about Chad. We hope to find his base of operations soon. The whole situation has to be handled delicately because of the power these men hold. When you feel better, Cole will need to speak with you and have you sign an affidavit. As soon as he narrows down Bob's properties that contain swamplands and gets your affidavit, he'll be able to apply for a warrant to search both Bob's property and the senator's."

"Soon." She wanted to do it soon. She wanted to see them all thrown in jail and wanted peace for the families of those missing women. She suddenly felt very tired. The sleeping pill was definitely working. She looked at Mo and pushed the tray toward him. He took her signal and handed the tray to Ahmed as he left.

"Come here. Let me hold you for a while. You can sleep knowing you are safe in my arms." Mo kicked off his shoes and slipped into bed. He held his arms open as she laid her head against his chest. Then he wrapped his arms around her and she fell asleep listening to the steady rhythm of his heart.

The next time she opened her eyes, she found Tammy and Paige sitting in chairs that had been placed beside the bed. They were looking at Tammy's phone. Dani turned her head to the side looking for Mo and heard the girls gasp.

"Oh, Dani! How are you feeling?" Paige scooted her chair closer to the bed.

"Throat hurts," she managed to get out. Her throat was so dry. Every time she swallowed, it felt as if sandpaper were being dragged down her throat. Paige jumped up and poured a glass of water into a small crystal glass.

"Here you go."

Dani took a sip and smiled. It felt so good that she drained the glass in three sips. "Where's Mo?" She looked around the room again, surprised he wasn't there.

"He and your parents are meeting with Cole and Ahmed. So we volunteered to keep you company." Tammy jumped up and moved the heavy chair forward. "And we have so much to tell you!"

Dani smiled. Contrary to her first thoughts, she apparently needed the perky little girl around her. She was already feeling better as she watched Tammy fluttering around.

"First, wow, what a house! Second, wow, what a man!" Paige laughed as she opened the heavy window curtains.

"Can't argue with that." Dani pushed up on her hands and scooted back against the mountain of pillows. "If you can get me some more water, then I'd love to hear all the news from town."

"Of course!" Tammy jumped up and grabbed the water pitcher. "We were all at the fair when we heard. The Roses jumped Red and made him bring them in the cruiser. That's how they got there so fast. They were like avenging angels when they heard the news."

"They were such a comfort. I think I'd have gone into shock without them there." Not wanting to be weighed down by talk of what happened with Chad, Dani looked away from the girls and tried to push the picture of his dead body back in her mind.

"Enough of that, Tammy. Tell her the fun stuff," Paige said. Dani turned her head when she felt Paige slip her hand into hers and squeeze. "And she has pictures."

"This sounds promising. Do tell."

"Well, I was early for my shift at the bake sale. So I went over to the stockyards. It's where they have bull riding, horse shows, pig wrestling, and so on." Tammy climbed onto the bed and sat cross-legged next to Dani. She pulled out her camera and pulled up the playback. "Guess who I caught at the pig wrestling contest?"

Dani looked at the small screen and stared as she tried to figure out the picture. There was a tall man with undeterminable hair color under all the mud. He was shirtless and had a nice body. But he was covered, literally from head to toe in mud and something shiny.

"What's the shiny stuff?"

"Vaseline. Gotta get the pig slick. Then you have one minute to catch it and move it to the holding pen over there. Can you tell who that is?"

Dani looked harder at the picture. He seemed familiar, but she just couldn't tell. The squirming pig in his arms prevented her from really being able to focus on him. "I'll give you a hint. Those slacks are not only shiny because of the Vaseline. And he was trying to impress the really cute girl who owned the pig."

"Henry?" Dani's mouth fell open as she stared harder at the picture. Paige and Tammy started to giggle. "No way! We have to get a very large print of this picture and hang it up in the office."

Dani shook her head and laughed in disbelief. She flipped to the next picture and laughed even harder. It was a picture of Henry, face down in the mud with the pig scrambling over his head to escape. She hit the button again and the image of a very handsome young man on a bull came onto the screen.

"Who's this?" Dani showed Tammy the picture.

"I don't know, but isn't he dreamy?" She sighed and pushed the button for another picture to come up. This one was a closer shot of the bull rider. His black cowboy hat was low on his head, covering his eyes. Dani could make out a strong jaw covered in brown stubble and a crooked nose, probably the result of being thrown a couple of times. Dani coughed and the sandpaper burn was back. Tammy jumped off the bed and grabbed the water pitcher. It was empty so she went into the bathroom to refill it.

"Let me see the cowboy," Paige said as she took Tammy's seat on the bed. "Oh!"

"Oh, what?"

"I know that cowboy," Paige grinned.

"You going to tell me or wait until I lose my voice completely?"

"It's my brother."

Dani rolled her eyes and held up her hand and wiggled her five fingers indicating Paige's five brothers.

"Sorry. I forget not everyone can tell them apart. That's my baby brother, Pierce." Dani choked and laughed until her voice went out. "You okay? What's so funny?"

Dani gestured for Paige to come closer so she didn't have to talk as loud. "Tammy said he was a band geek."

Paige broke out into peals of laughter and Dani now saw why Miles and Marshall had found it so funny. She looked at the picture again. She couldn't tell how tall he was. But if you can look that good while riding a bucking bull, who cares? He was solid muscle and the fit of his jeans definitely showed him to be a man, not a skinny scarecrow like Tammy thought.

"What's so funny?" Tammy walked out of the bathroom with a full pitcher of water. She poured Dani a glass and handed it to her. Dani could only shake her head and look at Paige.

"It'll be better for you to find out on your own. It would ruin the surprise." Turning to Dani, "Mo said we were to feed you and then pop another pill in you if you woke up. He said you are partial to ice cream. You want some?" Dani nodded and Paige got up and used the phone to call up some ice cream.

Dani listened to more stories from the fair as they all ate ice cream. Despite her best efforts, her eyes got heavy and closed all on their own. She'd have to have Tammy finish her story at work on Monday.

When she next opened her eyes, she found the bedroom awash in bright sunlight. She rolled onto her side and looked for Mo, only to discover he wasn't in the room. She stretched and noticed her throat wasn't in as much pain today. Tired of lying in bed, she swung her feet off the side and sat up. She waited for the nausea but was rewarded with only a slight headache. She found herself to be a little wobbly when she stood. She kept a hand on the bed as she walked toward the bathroom. Her mind was on one thing, a shower. She reached the bathroom and turned on the hot water. She unbuttoned her shirt and stepped under the spray. Muscles relaxed as the spell she had been living under for the past couple days wore off and her energy started to return.

She toweled off and did a quick blow-dry of her hair. Slipping into the pair of jeans she found folded in the bathroom, she went in search of another of Mo's shirts. She found a light-green shirt and buttoned it up. Next, she went in search of Mo. She headed downstairs and glanced into the rooms as she passed by. Heading into a part of the house she hadn't been into yet, she found a large dining room and a library. At the end of the hall, she opened a door and walked into a beautiful solarium. Vase after vase lined the back windows. Each vase held a dozen roses of red, yellow, white, pink, and purple.

Her breath caught as she realized that each vase had a letter drawn on them. As she looked down the line of flowers, she read, "Will you marry me?" One of her hands covered her open mouth, the other she placed on her rapidly beating heart as if she could slow it. She heard the door open behind her and slowly turned to see Mo walk in. His dark hair was brushed back and he looked breathtakingly handsome in his black pin-stripe suit.

"Danielle." He said her name like a prayer on his lips as he bent down on one knee before her. "My love. You have changed my world. I was lost and floating through life before meeting you. You have shown me true love and happiness. When you are not with me, I feel a part of me is missing. Make me whole. Say you will marry me and spend the rest of your life letting me show you just how much I love you."

"Yes!" She leaped into his arms when he rose. "I look forward to showing you just how much I love you, too."

Mo stepped back and reached into his pocket. He pulled out a black velvet box, opening it to show her a teardrop-shaped diamond.

"Oh, Mo! It's beautiful."

He took the ring out of the box and slipped it on her finger. "A perfect fit, just like us."

"I have to go tell my parents! I can't believe it! We're engaged!"

"Your parents know. I asked your father's permission the first night I met him. I was just waiting for the perfect time to ask you. When I almost lost you, I didn't want to wait any longer. I planned a celebratory lunch, if you are feeling up to it."

"This is why I love you! But what about your parents?"

"I have invited them to dinner. And that is why I love you." He leaned over and kissed her gently. She could tell he was still afraid of hurting her. She threw her arms around his neck and kissed him for all she was worth.

"I want to do the tests right now."

"What?"

"The tests that need to be done to announce the formal engagement. Can they be done now?"

"No. You are in no condition for them. I won't let you."

"Mohtadi, I will do them now or not at all." She placed her hands on her hips and refused to budge.

He held up hands in defeat and kissed her cheek, "Fine. I will call the doctors. It will make me feel better to know you are alright after Friday."

"Thank you. I want to be able to face your parents tonight with all of that behind me." She dropped her hands from her hips and gave him a hug. She stepped back as he pulled out a cell phone from his inside pocket. He stepped away from her and talked into the phone for a minute.

"The doctor and his staff will be here in thirty minutes. I will be right by your side through the whole thing. Like I told you before, there will be a physical exam. They will take some blood for a series of tests. Then he will ask you some questions, talk about your life growing up, and how you are handling this week's events. He will also ask about your views on life in the public eye. Are you sure you're up for it?"

"Yes, I'm sure. I really want to do this. I am not worried. It'll be a great relief to get it over with and make our engagement official."

"Come on, let's go upstairs and continue our celebration while we wait for the doctor to arrive."

The tests weren't as bad as she thought. They had drawn her blood and sent it out to be tested for hereditary diseases. She was told her arm was healing, but the violent bruising would take a couple more weeks to go down. Her head looked good and she'd start feeling better every day. Mo was handed a formal evaluation on her physical and mental health to submit to his father. She was cleared to be a princess. She still couldn't quite wrap her mind around it. Mo had never acted like typical royalty. To her, he was just Mo.

They walked hand in hand down the staircase and into the small, informal dining room. She let go of Mo's hand as she catapulted herself into her mother's arms.

"Can you believe it, Mama?" She held out the ring for her mother to exclaim over while her father shook Mo's hand and clasped his back.

"It's been a pleasure working with you in the past. I guess this means I must donate more wine to that charity of yours." Her father laughed and then turned to Danielle. "My *bambina*. How are you old enough to be getting married?" He wrapped her up in a hug and kissed the top of her head. "You chose well. You'll be very happy with him, as I am with your mother."

Mo came to stand beside her and placed his hand on the small of her back. "Why don't we sit down? I don't want you getting too tired for tonight." He held out a chair for her as he directed her parents where to sit.

The food was brought out from the kitchen and Dani's stomach did a happy jig when she smelled the lasagna and garlic bread. Mo raised his glass of wine. "To my new family. *Salute!*"

"*Salute!*" the table replied.

Her mother served the lasagna, her father poured the wine, Mo passed the bread, and Dani sat back to enjoy the sight of her family together. She ate a couple of bites. As her stomach filled, her eyes drooped.

"Please, Mary, Tony, enjoy the éclairs." Mo rose and walked over to her. "I am going to put Dani to bed."

Her mother scooted her chair back and came over to Dani. She placed a kiss on her cheek. "Sleep well, Bella. We will see you tonight."

Her father kissed her other cheek and gave her hand a little squeeze before Mo helped her out of her chair and walked her upstairs. She fit so perfectly in the crook of his arm. She inhaled his scent and her lids closed. When they opened again, he was lying her down in bed.

"I will wake you up for dinner. Sleep well, my love."

"Stay with me, please." She just wanted to feel him, to be near him.

"Of course." He kicked off his shoes and climbed into bed with her. Before he could even settle in, she fell asleep.

Dani brushed her long hair one more time. She knew she was doing it because of nerves. Mo had left fifteen minutes ago with the letter from the doctor and was meeting his parents in his study. She looked again in the mirror and adjusted her shawl to make sure it covered the bruises on her arm. A couple of layers of make-up had covered the bruise on her head. She couldn't do anything with the surgical tape except try to keep it covered with her hair. She took a deep breath and walked downstairs.

"Oh! My baby girl is all grown up!"

"Mama, I've been grown up for a decade," Dani rolled her eyes and smiled.

"To a mother, her daughter is never all the way grown up. You just have grown-up moments, and this is one of them." Her mother hugged her and kissed both of her cheeks. "Bella! You're freezing. Are you alright?" she asked.

"I'm fine, Mama. Just nervous. I've already met Mo's father once and he didn't like me very well."

"How could he not like you?" her father asked, as if it were impossible.

"He thought I was trying to marry Mo for his money and title. He, um, saw my car and made his mind up based on assumptions."

"How many times have I told you to get rid of that piece of junk? Didn't you tell him you are a very rich young lady with no need to marry into money?" Her father waved his arms around as if he still couldn't comprehend someone not liking her.

"No, Papa. I shouldn't have to defend myself like that. He was insulting and I don't think I needed to explain my financial situation as he was yelling at me." Dani's hands moved to her hips at the same time her father moved his hands to his.

"Enough. Both of you. Bella, I understand why you didn't say anything to him about your trust fund. Tony, you have to respect your daughter's decision not to be some air-headed heiress throwing her money about like it grew on trees." Her mother stared them down until they both removed their hands from their hips. "Now, with that said, I think we need to teach Mo's father a little something about manners. Come with me." Her mother turned, leaving Dani scrambling to keep up with her.

"What are you doing, Mama?"

"Turning you into an heiress." Her mother led Dani into her bedroom and opened the closet. "First, take off that dress and put this on." Her mother handed her a deep-green silk wrap dress that hit just above her knees. "Now, turn around so I can put this on."

Dani turned around and her mother draped a large diamond and emerald necklace across her bruised throat. The necklace would definitely draw the attention away from some of the darkness of the bruises she couldn't cover up.

"Perfect. Now let me put your hair up into a quick French twist and you'll teach Mo's father a lesson on judging people." Her mother deftly twisted her hair up and pinned her dark locks with a black and green clip. "Great. Now let's go meet your future in-laws."

Mo stood in the hallway when Dani made her way down the stairs with her mother. The look on his face was enough to boost the confidence his father had worn down.

"You look stunning. I am the luckiest man in the world."

He took her hand and placed it in the crook of his arm. He led the group to the formal sitting room. She took a final deep breath as he opened the door. The furniture was stiff and elegant. It looked like it belonged in Buckingham Palace, not Keeneston, Kentucky. The antique chairs and settees were covered in white silk with inlaid mahogany floors polished so well she could see her reflection. She put a smile on her face and lifted her head as she walked into the room.

"Danielle, may I present my father, His Royal Highness, Emir Ali Rahman," he introduced the regal-looking man in an Armani suit. His black-and-white beard and hair was freshly trimmed.

"Nice to see you again, sir." Dani boldly held out her hand. He rose and ignored her. Her heart plummeted and her cheeks flamed with embarrassment.

"Mohtadi, explain yourself. You told us you were marrying that money-grubbing parasite of a girl I met the other day. Then you walk in here with Tony De Luca and this beautiful woman I can only guess to be the heiress of De Luca Winery. What game are you playing and why are you bringing my old friend into it?"

If Dani wasn't so shocked, she'd laugh out loud. The collective gasp that came from her, her mother, and Mo would've been hilarious if she hadn't looked over at her father and saw him shake hands with Mo's father. Now she was just confused.

"Emir," her father said as they shook hands. "May I introduce my daughter, Danielle Isabella Darina De Luca. Also known as the money-grubbing parasite." Her father's voice was cold as ice as he stared down a king for her. She couldn't love her father any more than she did right then. She also knew her future husband would do the exact same for his children. Then she did smile.

"As I said, it's nice to see you again, sir." She didn't give him a second look as she turned to the beautiful woman dressed in a pale pink dress. "You must be Mo's mother. It is such a pleasure to meet you." She held out her hand and watched as his mother's face went from confusion to a large smile.

"Fatima Ali Rahman. I am so looking forward to having you in the family. Emir, isn't there something you would like to say to your future daughter?"

Everyone turned and stared at him. "I must beg your forgiveness at my rude assumptions from the other day. I hold Tony's friendship close to my heart and nothing will give me greater joy than to make us family."

"Thank you. You apology is accepted. Now, I'm dying to know how my father knows you and why he failed to mention it until now."

"I was wondering the same thing. Dear?" Dani's mother turned to her father and gave him The Look.

"Well, Emir fell in love with our wine. We met at his request after he bought some of the 1997 bottles. We've been friends ever since," her father explained. "As for not saying anything, I thought the fact I didn't kill Mo when he put his hands on you was enough of an acknowledgment of who he was and who his father was. After all, I gave him my consent to marry you that day, even after the way we met."

Emir laughed and put his arm around Tony. "We need a toast. To family, friends, and my new daughter!"

# Chapter Seventeen

---

Dani awoke to the feel of a hand sliding between her legs. "Mmm." She rolled over and didn't bother pulling up the covers over her naked body. She had decided sheets like Mo's were made for sleeping naked. His mouth closed on one of her nipples and thoughts of sheets and everything else fell away.

"I have to go, love." She watched as Mo disentangled himself from her and the sheets. "I have meetings with my father this morning. They should last most of the day. What is your schedule like?"

"Kenna is going to be back at the office and we have court this morning. I'll be going with her to help with the issues since she's been gone." She stretched and felt the happy afterglow left only by great sex. "How about we ditch them both and just stay in bed all day?"

"If only. Unfortunately, the United States and Canada will have officials at this meeting. I already postponed it once and I don't want to lose out on this contract."

"Kenna will be lost in court today if I'm not there. And I have to see if she'll be my matron of honor! I can't wait to tell the girls!" She jumped out of bed and ran to the shower.

"What kind of fiancé would I be if I didn't help you get ready for work?" Mo said as he stepped into the shower behind her.

"Ahmed, can't you go any faster?"

"No."

"Come on. Let me drive then."

"No."

"Ahmed, when I marry Mo, will I be your boss?"

"No."

"You're full of conversation today. You want to talk about it?"

"No."

Dani blew a piece of hair out of her eye and smiled at the purple Pradas Kenna had given her.

"But, I do owe you congratulations. I am very happy to have the privilege of being the head of your security as well."

"Thanks, Ahmed. I'm more excited about having you as a friend than as an employee." Finally, Ahmed smiled. She wondered what put him in such a snit. "Are you sure you don't want to talk about whatever it is that is bothering you. Is it a girl?" By the blush and the non-answer, Dani guessed she had hit the mark. "No way! You have a girlfriend?"

"No."

"Ugh! Can't you say anything else?" Ahmed just smiled and pulled up to the law office.

"Have a good day."

Dani shook her head, got out of the silver Mercedes, and headed inside. The front door hadn't even closed when Tammy jumped out of her seat.

"Oh my God, you're engaged! Look at that rock!"

Dani heard footsteps in the hallway as Kenna and Henry ran to the lobby.

"What did I hear? You're engaged and you didn't tell me!" Kenna grabbed her hand and examined the ring. "Nice! Congratulations!" Kenna hugged her tight. "I missed you."

"Sure you did. I'm guessing I was the last thing you were thinking about on your honeymoon." She gave Kenna a wink before Tammy threw herself at her for a hug.

"You haven't married him yet. I still have a chance." Henry said as he moved in for a congratulatory hug.

"Henry."

"Yes?"

"Get your hands off my ass."

"You women are no fun once you get engaged." He pouted and then walked back to his office.

"I have to call Paige. We'll have lunch after court to celebrate and I want every single detail! Nice shoes, by the way." With a smile, Kenna ran back to her office to call Paige.

Dani stopped by her office and picked up the printouts of all the case law she had done. The police had been there and a professional cleaner had put in new carpet. Everything was back to where it belonged. It was like it had never happened. She stared at the floor where Chad's dead body had fallen just days ago.

"I'm so sorry, Dani. I should've thought how hard this would be for you. I got carried away with your good news and nearly forgot about all that happened." Kenna slipped her arm around Dani and joined in staring at the blank floor.

"How are you doing?"

"Okay."

"No, really. How are you doing?"

"Not so hot now. I was okay at home. Now, standing here, I just can't stop reliving it."

"Let's get you a new office then. For now, let's just get to court and spread the gossip about the world's most eligible bachelor being engaged."

"Sounds good." She walked around the far side of the desk to avoid where the fight took place and opened her drawer. She pulled out her notes, stuffed them into her bag, and headed for the door, never taking a second glance at the place she had killed a man.

"There are my heroes." Dani grabbed Dinky and placed a big kiss right on his lips. She watched his face turn the same color red as the lipstick stain she left. She turned and kissed Noodle as well. "Is my case closed or are you going to be arresting me?"

"No, ma'am. We wouldn't do that. We closed it out on Friday. Self-defense. Everyone is right happy about it, too. It must be a big relief for you both."

"I hate that Dani had to go through it alone, but I must admit it does feel good knowing that bastard is dead." Kenna walked with Dani and Noodle up to the table before the bench and started laying out folders for the hearings.

"Welcome back, Kenna. I hope you…oh my gosh! Is that an engagement ring?" Martha all but shouted. Heads turned and Noodle blatantly stared as Martha picked up Dani's left hand. "Holy smokes. The sheik gave this to you?" Not waiting for an answer, she continued. "I bet that is going to be one heck of a wedding. I better call my daughter. She'll be crushed. She tried to catch his eye a couple of times, but I guess he was already focused on you. Congratulations!" Martha headed out the courtroom telling every person she saw about the engagement.

"I give it three minutes until every phone line in the county is busy spreading this news. So, what have we got today?"

Dani sat in the chair at the table and handed Kenna the files with a little note on the ones that were more complex. She enjoyed seeing her research pay off when someone who really deserved a second chance got one. Or, subsequently, when someone who had been handed third and forth chances got what they deserved. Dani sat back in her chair and watched the wheels of justice turn. The court was packed today after many of the cases from last week had been passed to this week so Kenna could try them.

She listened to the lawyers trying to strike deals with Kenna in last-ditch efforts to keep their clients from jail. She watched Noodle and Dinky trade off bailiff duties and the clerks entering all the information into the computers. She watched the judge work his way through the docket. And she watched the pile of files in front of

Kenna dwindle. Finally, the last case was before the judge. She knew it couldn't be good when Kenna rolled her eyes.

"Case Number 11-C-532, State vs. Tony Chapman. All parties wanting to be heard please come forward." Dinky yelled into the crowded courtroom.

Dani watched as a geek-looking man with light-red hair in his mid-twenties came forward. Behind him, a stern-looking woman with a simple brown dress followed. His attorney, a tall, slick man, met his client up at the podium.

"Mr. Chapman. Good to see you again. Who'd you expose yourself to this time?" Kenna asked.

Dani looked around the courtroom and found a kid, no more than eighteen or so, in the standard khaki pants and polo shirt with a bank logo, walk toward Kenna.

"Go ahead, Miss Mason." Judge Cooper already looked like he was trying to stop laughing.

"Mr. Chapman, it looks like you've engaged in public masturbation again. Why don't you just tell us what happened at the bank on June 24, 2011?"

"Well, I was in the drive-thru line at the bank to deposit a check and got bored. I didn't think anyone could see me."

"Mr. Chapman, are you aware there are cameras at every station?"

"No. I thought I could finally not get caught. Ever since the last time we were here, my wife has stopped wearing colors and won't even let me kiss her. On top of that, she makes me see Father James twice a week for sex addiction. How can I have a sex addiction if she won't even let me have sex?"

"Mr. Chapman, your sex life, or lack thereof, is not a legal defense for exposing yourself in public again," Kenna explained to him. Dani had a hard time not laughing, but at the same time one look at the wife and she felt sorry for him.

"Your Honor, my client is willing to spend a week in jail and will promise to move out of the marital home," Mr. Chapman's attorney said.

"And what does him promising to move out mean in terms of his sentence?" Kenna asked. Judge Cooper was thinking the same thing by the way his bushy eyebrows shot up.

"With Mr. Chapman maintaining a separate residence from his wife, he'll have the freedom to masturbate in the confines of his home and will have no more need to do so in public places."

Dani watched as both Kenna and Judge Cooper nodded their heads in agreement. Kenna talked to the attorney for a few more minutes, apparently hammering out the details.

"Your Honor, the State will agree to these terms."

"Okay. Mr. Chapman. If I find you in this court again, you will become a sex offender. So make sure you keep it in your pants outside of your home. Got it?"

"Yes, sir."

"The bailiff will take you into custody now. Say your goodbyes. You'll be out in a week. Okay, that's lunch." Judge Cooper pounded his gavel and everyone stood up.

Kenna hurried over as Dani slipped some files into her briefcase. "Come on, let's go see Paige and get a seat before everyone else gets over there. I can't wait to hear all about what has been going on. I can't believe I leave for one week and come back to find you engaged to the most eligible bachelor in the world! By the way, did I mention those are great shoes," Kenna winked at her.

"Thank you. I just had to wear them today. I've never been happier, but it started off pretty bumpy. His father definitely thought I was a gold digger until he discovered I was one of his friends' daughters. His face was priceless!"

"Have you made any plans yet?"

"Not yet. We don't want to wait long, though. My parents are here for the remainder of the month. I never knew such happiness was possible. I feel like a giddy school girl," she laughed as she pushed open the double glass doors and walked out into the parking lot.

"This is so great! I can't wait to talk wedding details!" Kenna slung her arm around Dani's shoulder and pulled her near as they started across the parking lot. "Look! There's Paige." Dani looked to where Kenna pointed and waved when she saw Paige.

Before she could put her hand down, two loud bangs reverberated off the old brick buildings. Dani looked to Kenna and saw her lying on the ground. She saw that Kenna wasn't moving as blood quickly spread across her chest. She tried to scream Kenna's name, but she couldn't make her mouth open.

She tried to scream again, but she couldn't breathe. It felt like a hot poker had stabbed her and sucked out all of the air. She looked down at her hand pressed against the side of her chest. She felt nothing as she saw the red blood pouring from between her fingers. She pulled her hand back to see what was wrong, but could only see her hand covered in her blood. She tried one more time to scream her fears but was engulfed in blackness.

Can't wait to read Paige's story? Then don't! *Dead Heat* is now available as an e-book in all outlets and in paperback on Amazon.com.

## Dead Heat

In the third book of the Bluegrass Series, Paige Davies finds her world turned upside down as she becomes involved in her best friend's nightmare. The strong-willed Paige doesn't know which is worse: someone trying to kill her, or losing her dog to the man she loves to hate.

FBI Agent Cole Parker can't decide whether he should strangle or kiss this infuriating woman of his dreams. As he works the case of his career, he finds that love can be tougher than bringing down some of the most powerful men in America.

And now introducing the **Bluegrass Brothers** series. This series will follow the Davies Brothers and the rest of the Keeneston crew through a new series of adventures.

## Bluegrass Undercover

Cade Davies had too much on his plate to pay attention to newest resident of Keeneston. He was too busy avoiding the Davies Brothers marriage trap set by half the town. But when a curvy redhead lands in Keeneston, the retired Army Ranger finds himself drawn to her. These feelings are only fueled by her apparent indifference and lack of faith in his ability to defend himself.

DEA Agent Annie Blake was undercover to bust a drug ring hiding in the adorable Southern town that preyed on high school athletes. She had thought to keep her head down and listen to the local gossip to find the maker of this deadly drug. What Annie didn't count on was becoming the local gossip. With marriage bets being placed and an entire town aiming to win the pot, Annie looks to Cade for help in bringing down the drug ring before another kid is killed. But can she deal with the feelings that follow?

# About the Author

Kathleen Brooks has garnered attention for her debut novel, *Bluegrass State of Mind,* as a new voice in romance with a warm Southern feel. Her books feature quirky, small town characters you'll feel like you've known forever, romance, humor, and mystery all mixed into one perfect glass of sweet tea.

Kathleen is an animal lover who supports rescue organizations and other non-profit organizations whose goals are to protect and save our four-legged family members.

Kathleen lives in Central Kentucky with her husband, daughter, two dogs, and a cat who thinks he's a dog. She loves to hear from readers and can be reached at Kathleen@Kathleen-Brooks.com.

Check out the Kathleen Brooks's Website, www.Kathleen-Brooks.com for updates on in the Bluegrass Series. You can also "Like" Kathleen on Facebook (facebook.com/KathleenBrooksAuthor) and follow her on Twitter @BluegrassBrooks.